Sign up for our newsletter to hear
about new releases, read interviews with
authors, enter giveaways,
and more.

www.ylva-publishing.com

— Twice Told Tales —

the *Secret* of
Sleepy Hollow

Andi Marquette

Acknowledgements

There's always more than an author behind a published story. I'd like to thank Astrid Ohletz of Ylva Publishing who saw something in this tale and welcomed me and *The Secret of Sleepy Hollow* into the Ylva family. Thank you, Astrid, for your initial suggestions regarding re-writes and for all you do for authors you bring on board. I'd also like to extend a hearty thanks to Joanie Bassler, who did the line edit and copyedit of *Sleepy Hollow* with patience and precision. She made this a stronger manuscript, and I am grateful for her efforts. Glendon and the crew at Street Light Graphics do a lot of work on interior and exterior/cover design, and *Sleepy Hollow* was no exception. Thanks to all of you. My gratitude, as well, to everyone at Ylva. Many of you wear many different hats, but no matter which hat it is, I know you're expending time, energy, and passion in what you're doing, and I appreciate every bit of it.

And many, many thanks to you, the reader, for joining me on another adventure. So sit back, and let me tell you a story...

Tales

ABBY PARKED IN A SPACE practically in front of the Sleepy Hollow Historical Society, a one-story unremarkable brick building with a plain glass door. It blended well with the other structures, a mixture of brick and clapboard. The city fathers probably wanted to maintain a quaint, small-town charm in addition to the appeal of the village's historical significance, which included its paranormal allure.

Abby picked up the book from the passenger seat and opened it to the page she'd flagged with a Post-it note, to the story in this collection that teased her some days, haunted her others. How many times had she read this damn story, looking for clues to her own history? The title seemed to both mock and entice her. "The Legend of Sleepy Hollow." Did Washington Irving have any idea, when this story was published in 1820, how it would wend its way into the American psyche? How the legend of the headless horseman in this corner of New York and the disappearance of Ichabod Crane would spawn first, speculation and later, movies?

She doubted it. No writer imagines that, even though Irving got a taste of it when he was alive, enjoying acclaim in the States and Europe. Abby flipped through the pages until she came to the first appearance of Katrina van Tassel, daughter of Baltus, one of the wealthiest men in Sleepy Hollow in the late 18th century. The Van Tassels were one of the founding families here, and when Ichabod arrived in 1799, Katrina immediately caught his attention.

And then he disappeared one October night. Irving left this event open to speculation. Was it the headless horseman that haunted the area since the Revolutionary War who caused it? Or a cruel joke perpetrated by another of Katrina's suitors, Abraham van Brunt, known as Brom Bones? Regardless, Ichabod disappeared in Irving's story and from the historical record, leaving behind the legend of the headless horseman. And, Abby thought, lots and lots of questions.

She got out of the car, still holding the book, and stretched. Though the late afternoon sun was warm, she grabbed her sweatshirt out of the back seat and put it on. This late in October, Abby knew the evening would be cool. Her laptop bag was on the floor behind the driver's seat and she slipped the book into it then slung the bag over her shoulder and locked the car.

An elderly man strolled past with a tiny dog dressed in an equally tiny blue sweater. He nodded at her and she smiled back. The dog glanced once at her, but clearly wasn't interested in stopping for a pat from a stranger. It had other business to conduct, like sniffing a nearby tree, whose leaves were a blaze of fall colors.

Abby approached the historical society and hesitated at the front door, her attention caught by a poster hanging on it below the open sign. The poster advertised the Sleepy Hollow Halloween festival, which was this weekend. The graphics included a creepy bridge, jack o' lanterns, and a galloping horse whose rider had no head. She stared at it for a few moments and thought about Washington Irving, writing the story that would be the root of all of this hype, and the cause of her current fascination with American folklore. She wondered, if the horseman weren't tied up in her own family's history, would she care as much about Sleepy Hollow and its history? Probably not.

A soft tone like a doorbell sounded somewhere in the back when Abby entered, but it wasn't necessary because a woman stood at the counter, engaged with a stack of papers. She wore a faded denim shirt and her dark hair, streaked with gray, was pulled back from her face.

The woman looked up over the rims of her reading glasses and smiled. "Hi, there. How can I help you?" She took her glasses off and set them on the counter.

"Hi. I'm Abby Crane." Abby unfastened the clasp of her bag. "I made an appointment a month ago to do some research here and I confirmed with someone—I think it was Robert—on Monday." She pulled a business card out of her bag and handed it over.

"Of course. Ms. Crane." The woman picked up the card and glanced at it. "Tabitha." She looked back at Abby. "There's a name you don't see every day."

"It has yet to make a comeback," Abby said with a smile. She got a comment every time, when people realized her full name wasn't Abigail.

"It's a lovely name." She set the card on the counter. "You made the original appointment with me. I'm Luanne, but most everybody calls me Lu. How was your drive?"

"Fine. I just thought I'd come by before you closed to introduce myself." Abby re-fastened her bag.

"You didn't have to do that, but I do appreciate it. Where are you staying?"

"The Maple Tree Inn."

Lu smiled again. "Then you've already met Eleanor. She volunteers here. A font of information about local lore." The phone rang. "One moment," she said.

Abby nodded as Lu answered and used the time Lu was talking to have a look around. The interior of the building was sleek and modern, unlike its brick exterior. This was an older building, completely refurbished, and painted in a ubiquitous museum-style shade of white, but the track lighting created a warm and welcoming atmosphere.

Several display cases decorated the adjoining room, some on the walls and larger ones in the middle of the room. All but one held historic artifacts, including tools, daily implements, and explanatory cards that provided provenance and significance in the community. Sleepy Hollow was closely linked to Tarrytown. North Tarrytown had actually renamed itself Sleepy Hollow in 1996 in honor of Washington Irving's story. But the focus in this room was on the agricultural and manufacturing base of the city, made ideal because the Hudson River was so close. Plus, its natural beauty had drawn lots of people, including the elite. The Rockefellers had a house here.

The remaining display cases focused on prehistory, and included artifacts from the local Indian tribe that had occupied the area prior to white settlement. They'd done a good job setting it up, Abby thought. Someone had put a lot of thought into the choice of artifacts and how to display them, as well as what to write in the descriptions. It was better than some larger museums she'd been to.

She was about to go into the second room when Lu joined her.

"We've tried to ensure that we don't forget the people who were here in this area before us." Lu motioned at the prehistory case. "We maintain relationships with current tribes, and they graciously send us people to give talks throughout the year. Always well-attended, I might add." Lu slipped her hands into the back pockets of her jeans. "History is important in places like this. Many of the people currently living here can trace their roots back to the original settlement. And a few can trace to a tribe." A smile twitched at the corner of Lu's lips. "People are people," she said. "They tend to mix and mingle no matter what the conventional wisdom suggests. Of course, it's very different in some ways here now. We're a bedroom community for people who commute into Manhattan, but we're pleased that we've been able to maintain a small town sort of ethos."

Abby smiled back. She liked Lu's vibe. Professional but approachable. Abby guessed she, too, was serious about history. "Who did the displays here? They're great."

"All of us had a hand in them. Robert and Eleanor and a few other volunteers helped me with the artifacts. Robert's better with turns of phrase, so he did most of the informational cards. I did the brunt of the arranging within the cases."

Abby nodded. "They're really excellent."

"Good to know that graduate degree in museum studies I got paid off, eh?" Lu winked at her.

"So you're saying there's hope for me outside academia?"

Lu grinned. "You never know where life will take you. At any rate, the materials you've requested we keep in the vault." She laughed at Abby's expression. "That's what we call it. It's our climate controlled storage area. We bring materials up to the reading room."

"Wow. Could I see the storage area?"

"Certainly. Tomorrow morning. Go ahead and finish looking around. I have to do a few things before we close up. Let me know if you'd like a more in-depth explanation of anything."

"Thanks."

Lu returned to the counter and Abby walked slowly through the second room, which led to a small third room that was designed for showing films. Six long carpeted benches faced a blank screen. A sign explained that the movie—a documentary that provided an overview of the history of the area—showed every hour at the top of the hour and lasted twenty minutes. The last showing was at four each afternoon. Abby had arrived at four-thirty. Sometimes the short films at historical societies were informative. Other times, not so much. Maybe some day she'd do a documentary on Sleepy Hollow, and it would show here, too.

She moved to the display cases that she hadn't seen. One held her attention. "Ghostly Legends," the sign on this case said. A pen-and-ink drawing in the style of the eighteenth century depicted a man on a black horse. He was dressed in a uniform—presumably for war—and he held a long sword. The information card next to the drawing provided a short paragraph about him, and referred to him as "The Hessian."

Abby knew the legend by heart. This particular Hessian soldier had come to the Sleepy Hollow area, where he fought for American forces against the British in the Revolutionary War. He died, the legend suggested, when his head was shot off by a cannon ball during a battle and he rode after death, the headless horseman of Sleepy Hollow. She studied the drawing, but there was no indication in the man's features that he was the type of guy to ride long after death looking for his missing head. She'd always wondered why he'd want it back after a cannon ball got through with it. Seemed like a wasted effort. But there was no accounting for the motivations of ghosts, or, more importantly, the development of a great story.

She took the book out of her bag and reread Irving's description of Ichabod's encounter with the horseman. Gigantic in height, Irving had written, and the horseman's head rested on the pommel of his saddle. That's what he had thrown at Ichabod, the story went, and it hit him and then... he was gone, from the legend and the historical record.

Abby put the book back into her bag. The other ghostly legends included references to the Hollow as a place brimming with paranormal activity since the Dutch settled it. Another suggested an Indian medicine man may have been responsible for imbuing the area with lots of otherworldly powers. Regardless, the information cards said, "rumors of spectral sightings and strange occurrences are woven into the fabric of Sleepy Hollow."

Which made for a fascinating community study for her dissertation – how certain places were shaped by beliefs in paranormal phenomena that had become part of the local and regional history. It helped, of course, that she had an ancestor who was part of one of those legends.

Abby returned to the counter. "Thanks," she said to Lu. "See you tomorrow." She turned to go.

"Do you have plans for dinner?"

Abby stopped and looked over in surprise. "No, not really."

"Would you like to join me and Eleanor for a bite? You can get an earful of local lore. Some of it is true." She smiled.

"Sure."

"Wonderful. How about in an hour? You can walk to the restaurant with Eleanor. It's only a couple blocks from the Maple Tree."

"Sounds great. Thank you so much." Abby started for the front door, guessing that Lu probably wanted to close up.

"We historian-types love to chat each other up. See you soon." She closed the door behind Abby and flipped the sign to "Closed."

Abby returned to her car, but she didn't get in right away. Instead, she stood and admired the town. She looked back toward downtown, thinking that this could be a classic New England village postcard. A group of kids with backpacks had congregated outside what looked like a bakery across the street. Abby estimated them as junior-high age. Some of the trees that lined the street still retained their fall colors, rich reds and yellows trembling in the breeze. As Abby watched, a few let go of their moorings and fell to the sidewalks and street.

Banners for the annual Halloween festival hung over the street, attached to the black Victorian-style lampposts on either side. The closest one included a black horse rearing up on its hind legs in the banner's center, and its black-clothed rider held a leering jack-o'-lantern in his upraised hand. The rider had no head. A chill shot down her spine, a sense of expectation and something else she couldn't name.

"Will you stay for the celebration?" Lu asked, and Abby tore her gaze away from the picture on the banner to look at her. She had put on a jean jacket and had a backpack slung over one shoulder. She gripped the handles of a tote bag filled with books in one hand.

"I was planning on it, yes."

"It's quite a spectacle. Sort of a combined harvest festival and nod to Samhain, and we do have quite a frightening haunted house here in town. We have our own addition, of course." Lu looked at the banner. "The rider begins his rounds usually around eight-thirty or nine, so the younger kids can get a look at him before they go to bed. Depending on who it is, he'll ride for an hour or two, though a couple we've had in the past have gone a little longer than that."

"You mean you actually have a headless horseman?" Abby glanced at the banner again.

"Of course. It's Sleepy Hollow, after all. One of the locals volunteers every year."

"Where does he ride?" That was something she wanted to see. It would be a great addition to her research. A legend kept alive by a town's culture.

"All over. Mostly the outskirts, and through the real Sleepy Hollow glen. We're named for that, which is where all manner of ghostly things are alleged to happen. As I'm sure you know."

"Has anybody ever seen the real horseman?"

Lu gave her a mischievous smile. "Before or after he died?"

Abby grinned. "After."

"Yes. People have been seeing him since the Revolutionary War." Lu adjusted the backpack. "At least, they *claim* they've seen him. Others say they've heard his horse, galloping through the Hollow. They all lived to tell about it, clearly."

"Not all," Abby said and she looked up at the banner again. "According to legend." She turned her gaze back to Lu.

"Well, yes. There was one who disappeared, according to legend." Lu's expression turned quizzical. "Tabitha Crane," she said, as if testing the way it sounded. "I wondered when you first called to set up the appointment. What's your relationship to Ichabod?"

"He was a brother of my father's direct ancestor. A great-great-great-great uncle to me or something like that."

"Doing a bit of family history, then, in addition to your community study?"

"I thought it might be interesting, to see if I could find anything along those lines." She'd wondered, actually, most of her life what had happened to Ichabod.

"Well, you're in luck. Eleanor has been through our collection of the Van Tassel papers dozens of times."

"And the Van Brunt?"

Lu smiled. "We do have quite a bit of their papers, too. Eleanor helped catalogue them, but she's more familiar with the Van Tassel collection. But even in terms of the Van Brunt papers, she can probably point you in any direction you'd like to go."

"That would be great."

"And she loves talking history. You'll see for yourself. At any rate, I'll see you at the restaurant. I have to run home and drop a few things off." Lu lifted the tote bag just as an SUV drove past and its driver honked and waved at Lu, who waved back with her free hand. Abby caught a glimpse of the driver—female—and her dark hair and a flash of a smile.

Small towns, Abby thought. Everybody knew everybody else. "See you in a bit," she said to Lu as she opened her car and put her bag on the floor behind the driver's seat. She was looking forward to being able to walk most of the time while she was here, to get a real feel for the place. She slowly backed out of the space and headed down Main Street, toward downtown.

Dark and comfortable, the pub's walls were lined with booths, and several wooden tables in the center of the room provided other seating. About half the tables and booths were full, and Abby caught snippets of various conversations. She thought she heard "horseman" a couple of times.

A server walked past with someone's order, the smell of hot French fries lingering even after the food was delivered. The ceiling near the bar was plastered with coasters from a variety of beers and countries, many of which emphasized paranormal themes. A headless horseman appeared on a few.

"How much do you know about the local history of Sleepy Hollow?" Lu asked. She was seated across from Abby in this pub that was only a couple of blocks from the bed and breakfast.

"Not as much as I'd like to. There are the legends, of course, but the point of my research is to look behind those and see what might really have gone on, if anything. This is the first time I'm looking at the primary documents."

"Legends always have a grain of truth," Eleanor said. "But then people embellish. Like our dear friend Washington Irving." She smiled and took a buffalo wing from the plate in the center of the table. "He set his story around 1790, but the events of it happened around 1799. Creative license, of course."

Eleanor sat next to Lu, and Abby had guessed, when she checked in at the bed and breakfast earlier, that Eleanor was probably in her mid to late sixties. Her hair was nearly all white, and she kept it short. She wore a maroon turtleneck under a tan sweater and dark brown corduroys. She looked like she was ready to take off on a hike. From her great complexion and down-to-earth vibe, Abby figured she did that quite a bit.

"I guess I do wonder what happened to Ichabod and why he disappeared from the historical record," Abby said.

"Scandal," Eleanor said with a smile before she wiped her mouth.

Lu laughed. "El and I have our theories. We think the legend is correct insofar as there was something between Ichabod and Katrina van Tassel—you are familiar with the Van Tassel name in this area? Not just that it's a name on a collection of papers?"

Abby took another wing. "Dutch, one of the founding families, had money back in the day. Still a lot of Van Tassels around, and they're integral to Ichabod's story."

"The Van Brunts were influential, as well. Brom's— Abraham's family, from the legend." Lu sipped her iced tea. "At any rate, El and I think that Ichabod and Katrina were an item of sorts."

"And then Ichabod disappeared," Eleanor said, "and we're not sure what happened to him, as legend has it his body was never found."

"Not unusual," Lu interjected. "After all, his body could've been dragged off by a bear or some such. Depending on where he last was."

Abby moved her glass so the server could put her salad down. "I can't find any record of Ichabod after he disappeared. Not even in my family history. He was there, and then he wasn't."

"History can be maddening," Eleanor said as she picked up her Reuben. "That's why we love it so. Keeps us occupied for years. Do you have anything in particular you'd like to see in the Van Tassel or Van Brunt papers?"

"I think I'd like to start with the Van Tassels, and get a sense of them. Correspondence, business papers. That sort of thing."

"We have a wonderful collection of the correspondence, as I'm sure you know," Eleanor said. "Katrina—Baltus's daughter, from the legend—was a particularly lively writer. You'll find mention of Ichabod in her letters. Perhaps you'll see something that the rest of us haven't. Lu and I like to think that Katrina lived passionately."

Lu chuckled as she finished dressing her burger. "She did have a flare for the dramatic. But I don't want to spoil it for you," she said to Abby.

"So what's the deal with the horseman?" Abby asked.

"Oh, my. He is a primary figure in the legend of Ichabod Crane, but he's not the only story here." Eleanor wiped her hands off and sipped her wine.

"How so?" Abby asked.

"Well, I think the real force behind Ichabod's legend is the fact that he disappeared. Legend created a reason for that—a ghost horseman who was already established as part of the lore of this area. But the story behind Ichabod and Katrina is the one that I think drives the folklore. Something happened between them, and it culminated one night in 1799, at which point Ichabod was no longer part of the historical record. The blame for his disappearance fell on a ghost, which is always easy to do when perhaps you don't want to look inward or involve locals in an investigation."

"Are you suggesting he was murdered?" Abby set her fork down and reached for her iced tea. Irving had set that possibility up, and hinted that it might be Brom, but because the history was conjectural in that regard, so was the story.

"It's a possibility, but as you go through Katrina's correspondence in particular, I don't think that's what happened. But something did, and therein lies the mystery. The horseman is merely a vehicle for mysteries rather than a creator of them."

"The horseman is definitely tied to Ichabod's story in some way," Lu said. "But like El says, there's a much bigger story behind the horseman and Ichabod. What that is we aren't sure, but the horseman eventually took precedence over whatever really happened that night. After all, a headless ghost riding around a haunted glen has more sex appeal than a story about political and romantic intrigue, which often takes longer to unravel."

"So was there actually a Hessian soldier who could've been the source of the ghost horseman story?" Abby continued eating her salad.

"Yes," Eleanor said. "His history is correct in that there were Hessian soldiers in this area during the Revolutionary War. Many undoubtedly died in battle. Some were properly buried, with tombstones, and there's a record of them. Others, not so much. There was a mention of a Hessian soldier who suffered a terrible head injury in a battle near White Plains—"

"Sorry to interrupt, but where was this injury mentioned?" Abby asked.

"Well, let me think. Lu, do you remember?"

"One of the local manors in this area was used as a temporary medical facility, and one of the Van Brunts kept an inventory. It's in that collection. I recall that the injury killed the soldier, but they didn't include a name." She ate a fry. "And from that, it seems, came the headless horseman. But we're not entirely sure how or why."

"Weird, how that happens." Abby poked at a tomato. Somehow, a story grew from some unknown soldier's death into a driving force behind a ghostly legend that had repercussions in several families and in the history of a town.

"It is," Eleanor said. "Fascinating, isn't it? But I've always been curious about the love triangle between Katrina, Brom Bones, and Ichabod. I personally think Ichabod was her first choice, and when he disappeared, I think it may have devastated her. I always wonder what might have happened if Ichabod hadn't disappeared. Guess that's the romantic in me." She smiled at Abby.

"Regardless, if you decide to go through Katrina's correspondence, you may come to some conclusions about Ichabod," Lu said. "That's one of the things I enjoy about history so much, seeing the people I'm studying as human, with pain and love and joy and sorrow. That's what makes history come alive for me. So many things can change in terms of technology and politics and the like, but ultimately, we're all human."

Abby nodded. That was one of her favorite things about history, too. And she wondered, sometimes, about Ichabod and what happened to him. Maybe he was able to hook up with Katrina. Abby hoped he did, and that they were happy, if only for a while. Maybe she was a romantic, too, in spite of her completely unsuccessful dating experiences over the past year.

They finished the meal and Abby handed cash to Lu, who was going through the bill. "Thanks for inviting me."

"A pleasure," Lu said. "And rather interesting, having a Crane back in Sleepy Hollow."

"Yes. You're part of the legend, now," Eleanor said.

"What do you mean?" Abby stopped sliding out of the booth.

"Well, I don't believe I've ever met a Crane. At least not one who had a direct connection to Ichabod. It changes things."

"What things?" Abby remained in the booth, puzzled but also a little creeped out, though she wasn't sure why.

Eleanor smiled, which blunted the creepy factor. "There's just such a mystery surrounding Ichabod's disappearance. Katrina, I think, loved him passionately but when he disappeared, it left a gap in the historical record as well as in her life. Legends develop to fill those gaps, but I always wondered if perhaps Katrina never rested, and she's still out there, looking for him. Like Lu says, it's interesting, that a Crane shows up who happens to be a historian. Perhaps it's time for the mystery to be solved."

"That's a lot of responsibility when I'm just here to look at documents," Abby said. Eleanor might have spent way too much time with the legend, she decided.

"You never know what you're going to find. After all, you're a Crane who came looking. So now there are two Cranes in our local lore."

"Yeah, I guess so. Maybe history does repeat itself in some ways." Abby stood and put on her fleece jacket.

Eleanor got out of the booth and stepped aside so Lu could get out, too. "I'll meet you outside," Eleanor said. "Lu and I see someone over there we have to talk to."

Abby nodded and made her way between the tables toward the front door. The pub was by no means raucous, but it was busy for a Wednesday. Must be a favorite local hang-out, she guessed. She reached to push the front door open and someone on the other side pulled it at the same time. Abby stumbled a little across the threshold to the sidewalk beyond.

"Oh, sorry," said a woman outside, still holding the door open.

"It's okay." Abby straightened and looked at her. She had her dark hair pulled back in a ponytail and she wore jeans and a sweatshirt under a barn jacket. Abby stared, knowing it might be rude of her to do so, but unable to stop.

"My fault. I get a little too exuberant sometimes when I open doors." The stranger smiled and Abby kept staring because the smile was warm and welcoming and almost familiar, though Abby knew they'd never met.

"Hey, c'mon, K," said a guy behind the stranger. "Starving." He nodded at Abby and she nodded back as he brushed past her into the pub.

"He's starving," Abby said with a smile. "Better not let him into the kitchen unsupervised."

"Brothers," the stranger said with a laugh. "Have a great evening."

"You, too." Abby moved so the woman could go inside but she didn't and instead they stared at each other for a few more moments before the stranger broke the contact.

"Later," she said, with another little smile as she went inside.

Abby continued staring, this time at the door. Was there such a thing as an instantaneous crush? Because that's what it felt like.

Both Eleanor and Lu joined Abby outside. They said their good nights and Lu went the opposite direction from them. Two blocks later, Abby thanked Eleanor and went up to her room, tired from the drive and the day. She fell asleep soon after her head hit the pillow, thinking about the woman at the pub.

Secrets

WHERE WAS THIS PLACE? ABBY *smelled damp earth overladen with wet wood. A forest. She was in a forest enveloped by night and weak moonlight. She knew it was cold because she could see her breath, though she didn't feel the chill. Carefully, she took a step, then another.*

She heard a woman's voice drifting through the trees, but she couldn't make out words. Another step. And another.

"Ichabod."

Abby stopped. That, she heard. A woman, approaching. Abby heard movement in the forest but she couldn't tell what direction. She had to find the woman because the woman had something to tell her. Something important, but she wasn't sure what.

"Ichabod," whispered the woman again, much closer, but Abby still couldn't see her. She took two more steps, and then she heard hoofbeats, like a drum, all around her, coming from all directions. Where could she run? There was no escape. A big black shape burst into the clearing. A headless rider on a horse, wielding a sword. She couldn't move. The horse slowed to a walk and advanced on her, moonlight glinting off the buttons on the rider's uniform.

"Ichabod," called the unknown woman.

But Abby couldn't even turn toward the sound. She stared at the horse as it got closer and closer—

She sat up with a jerk. Morning light filled the room, and as she turned to look at the clock on her bedside table, the alarm buzzed. She turned it off and rolled out of bed, glad it was morning, glad it was only a dream.

But it stuck with her through her morning shower and then breakfast and all the way to the historical society. Probably she'd dreamed it because she'd been talking about the legend the night before, and Eleanor's strange statements had left her a little uneasy.

And though Lu greeted her enthusiastically, Abby still couldn't shake the dream. Maybe getting focused on history would help. Sure enough, after Lu took her down into the climate-controlled vault on a tour, Abby felt a little better, and by the time she was back in the reading room with her first box of material, the effects of the dream had dissipated.

She set up her laptop for taking notes and opened the box, paying attention to how the files were arranged with labeled tabs indicating the order the archivist had assigned. Abby put on the white cloth gloves Lu had supplied. Though the documents were preserved in transparent sleeves, it helped keep the plastic clean and oil-free by wearing gloves. Part of the glamorous fashion of a historian, Abby thought as she withdrew the first file, which dealt mostly with business according to the collections list.

The first document was an inventory, written in black ink in a cramped, neat script. The paper was in good shape. Abby held it up to the overhead lights. It was good quality, from the look of the fibers. Not easy to get back in the day, but the wealthy managed to acquire it. She imagined Baltus sitting down at his writing desk, dipping his quill into the inkwell, and painstakingly writing out his inventory. Or rather, whoever he designated to do it. As she skimmed the list of items, Abby guessed that Baltus was exacting, and probably would check and double-check the items if he didn't do the inventories himself.

Well, nobody said all of history was exciting, Abby thought as she settled in and prepared herself to go through some more boxes.

A few hours later she finished going through her third box of Van Tassel papers. The routine of research had cleared out the rest of the dream, and now she was focused on figuring out what direction the collections were taking her and how the materials fit into her larger theme.

She checked the inventory list Lu had provided. Eleanor had suggested the Van Tassel papers first as good background for the community of Sleepy Hollow. She'd gotten a lot of excellent historical context thus far. The Van Tassels had been consummate record-keepers, right down to how much ink they used on a monthly basis. All of that was useful, historically speaking, but now she was ready to delve into some relationships. The fourth box, Eleanor had said, primarily held correspondence. She looked forward to exploring that one next.

Abby carefully returned the materials to the box, making sure they were in the order she had found them. She picked up the box and used her back to push the glass door of the reading room open before she continued on to the front counter, keeping her gaze on the floor. The reading room was in the back of the building, and Abby had to carry the box through the display area. It would not be pretty if she tripped carrying this box and scattered files and centuries-old documents all over the floor. As she rounded the corner to the counter, she nearly smacked into somebody.

"Oh, sorry," Abby said, but then she didn't say anything else as she stared into the other woman's eyes, a soft brown that crinkled at the corners as she smiled. She had her hair pulled back into a ponytail, like she had the night before, when Abby had thought she was cute. In daylight, she was even more attractive. And again, Abby was struck by a sense of familiarity.

"My fault," the stranger said with a laugh. "And we've got to stop meeting like this."

"It would probably be a good idea," Abby smiled back. "For public safety if nothing else."

"Good thing you have good balance. Lu and Eleanor would kill me if they knew I made you drop a Van Tassel box."

"How did—"

She pointed at the side of the box and the large black letters. "Kinda obvious."

Abby smiled back, sheepish. "Duh."

The newcomer laughed again, and it was a rich, fun-filled sound that lit little sparks in Abby's chest.

"I'm Katie. You must be Abby. You were out of context last night, or I would've introduced myself then."

"Yeah." And then she couldn't think of anything else to say, because it was a little disconcerting to have a reaction like that to someone she'd just met. "Um, I mean, yes, I'm Abby."

"Lu said you were coming in from UConn to do some research," she said, saving Abby from both her awkward silence and response. "I'm in grad school at Binghamton. Political science."

"Oh, cool. Are you on some kind of break?" Abby adjusted her stance. The box was heavy. Katie apparently caught the movement.

"Just a visit. Here. I'll go put this up." She reached for the box. "Did you want number four?" Her fingers brushed Abby's and the sparks left Abby's chest to race down her legs and up her arms.

"Yes. Thanks."

"That's mostly correspondence," Katie said.

"You've been through the collections?" Abby surreptitiously rubbed her fingers on her jeans to make them stop buzzing from Katie's inadvertent touch.

"Not in fine-tooth detail, but I'm familiar enough. I volunteered here in high school and undergrad years, and I help out when I'm in town."

Abby was about to respond when Katie turned and walked away. "Be right back with the other box," she said over her shoulder with another grin.

"Okay." Abby stared after her, admiring the way Katie's butt filled her jeans. She tore her gaze away and returned to the reading room, laughing at herself about her reactions. Even geeky historian grad students enjoyed a distraction now and again. But how weird, that the woman from last night was here at the historical society today.

Katie appeared at the door a few minutes later and Abby pushed it open for her.

"Here you go," Katie said. "Box four. Mostly Baltus's letters to businessmen, though there are some letters from family overseas." Katie set the box on the big wooden conference table. "And in the last few files you'll meet Katrina van Tassel—you know. Baltus's daughter—though you'll find out more about her in box five, which I think you'll enjoy more."

"What kind of letters did she write? Eleanor and Lu said she was pretty detailed."

"She was. And fun, for the most part. She was pretty observant."

"Who did she write to?"

"Relatives and friends, mostly. One of her cousins in New York City she was particularly close to." Katie leaned forward and lowered her voice, dramatic. "I think this cousin was a lesbian."

"Uh," Abby said because she wasn't sure what else to make of this revelation.

"I mean, insofar as the idea of a lesbian identity was understood back then."

"What makes you think that?"

Katie gave her a conspiratorial smile. "I don't want to bias you further. See if you come to the same conclusions. I'll catch up with you later. I'm interested to find out what you—as a historian—think."

"All right." Abby watched her go, enjoying another view of Katie's ass and wondering if Katie might have been throwing her a little clue about herself. With a sigh, Abby turned back to the box, put on her gloves, and dug into the first file. Katrina first. Then maybe she'd let herself think more about the effect Katie had on her.

Two hours later, Abby sat back, thinking. Many of the letters Katrina had written in English, though it had been difficult for Abby to get the hang of her script. Some were in Dutch, and she could figure those out from her own language background.

Katrina van Tassel had indeed written to friends and family and, as Katie had said, she'd written to a female cousin in New York City more often than to others, at least in terms of this box. Cousin Johanna hadn't mentioned men in her life beyond friends and brothers, but she spoke often of a "dear friend" Margaret, and Katrina asked after her in every letter Abby had thus far read.

Intrigued, she packed up box four and took it down to Lu. "I'm particularly interested in Katrina van Tassel's correspondence," she said as she placed the box carefully on the counter.

"Ah, yes. Boxes four through eight. I'll get five. That one has quite a lot of her letters." Lu took the box and disappeared into the back, to the stairs that would take her down to the vault. The most fragile documents remained there, and couldn't be examined in the reading room. Rather, they had to stay in the vault, and researchers were supervised while going through them. Abby didn't think she'd need to see any of those, but Lu had given her a list of what was included, in case she changed her mind.

"Box five," Lu announced, and Abby signed the sheet on the clipboard Lu had left on the counter. Eleanor had said last night that she recalled a mention of Ichabod in this box, in a letter Katrina had written to Johanna. Abby took the box back to the reading room, put her gloves on, and resumed working through the files. And soon, things got really interesting.

Katrina mentioned her displeasure about Abraham van Brunt, who was openly courting her in 1799. She considered him somewhat of a boor, according to her letters to Johanna, though she was more restrained in her opinions of him to other family members and friends. He was known around town as "Brom Bones," and she referred to him most often as Brom, like Lu and Eleanor did. "Dear Johanna," she wrote in English during the spring of 1799, "how I wish I could come live with you and Margaret in New York. Perhaps Brom would direct his designs elsewhere were I not present, though I know Father approves of him and his damnable attentions."

Abby typed the letter's date into her laptop along with the quote. So Johanna and Margaret lived together. Of course, they could be sisters. But if that were the case, why didn't Abby write to Margaret directly, as another cousin? She took the last file out of the box. Midway through the file while reading another of Katrina's letters, she stopped and re-read the previous paragraph.

There it was. The name Crane, on a letter dated from early summer, 1799. Katrina referenced a "Mr. I. Crane, of Connecticut." Abby's heart rate increased. For the first time, she was seeing her ancestor's name outside a story. According to the letter, Crane behaved like a gentleman in all accords, dressed simply but neatly, and was able to dance. Katrina described him as "handsome, delicate of feature, not very tall, and certainly not an oaf, as Brom is." He had come to teach at the local school, and Katrina marveled that he encouraged the girls in the village to come as well, much to the consternation of local officials.

"I'm afraid Mr. Crane has made an enemy of old Van Brunt the magistrate," Katrina wrote two letters later. "It seems he is much perturbed at Mr. Crane's insistence on ensuring all the girls in the village can read. He is quite odd, this Mr. Crane, but I find him an excellent and respectful conversationalist. And he truly is pleasant to look upon. I find myself drawn to him, much to my pleasure and chagrin. I anticipate seeing him each day, and long for his company when he is otherwise occupied, but I know such could never be. My father wishes to marry me into the Van Brunt family. I suppose I'm hoping that Brom's younger brother is less oafish than he, but there are several years between us."

The last letter in the file, dated in July, was Katrina writing to Johanna again. She started with the usual news from around the village but finished cryptically with, "I have discovered something, Johanna, and I'm certain both you and Margaret will be quite astounded at this revelation. It concerns Mr. Crane, who is not who we all thought him to be. Indeed, he is so much more. As I will be coming to New York next week, dear Johanna, I shall reveal what I know to you then. To wit, it explains quite a lot, and I am both elated but distressed."

Abby put the letter down. "What?" she asked the file. "What did you find out?" She looked through the letters in that file again, wondering if perhaps she had missed something. No, she hadn't. "Damn," Abby muttered as she put the file back in the box. "Come on, Katrina. What did you find out?" She made a note of the letter, the date, and the file just as Lu appeared at the door.

"I'm ready for box six," Abby said, needing to know what Katrina had found out.

Lu grinned. "It's nearly five." She pointed at the clock on the opposite wall.

Abby stared. She'd totally lost track of time. She'd even missed lunch.

"A true historian," Lu said. "Lost in time. Go get something to eat and get some rest. Box six will be here when you come back tomorrow." Lu checked through the files and Abby opened her laptop bag for inspection. She didn't mind the protocol. There were people out there, after all, who liked to steal historic documents. She wasn't one of them, but Lu didn't know that yet. Abby took her bag back from Lu and held the door for her, since she was carrying the box of files.

"Wait for me at the counter," Lu said. "I have something I think you'll enjoy reading."

A few minutes later Lu appeared from the back, carrying a white plastic binder. "Back in the nineties, one of our volunteers got interested in Ichabod. So she went through all of the letters between Katrina and Johanna, trying to piece together what happened to him. These are her findings." She handed the binder to Abby. "Go ahead and take it with you tonight. I've signed it out to you. It probably doesn't have much to do with your project overall, but it might give you some new directions for your family history."

"Excellent. Thanks." Abby put it in her laptop bag. "See you tomorrow morning."

"If you come before we open, you can have coffee and donuts with us in the break room. Robert might have some thoughts about your project."

"That would be great. What time?"

"Seven-thirty. Just call me on my cell when you get here. I'll come and let you in. Have a good evening."

Abby nodded and left, deciding she'd have dinner at the pub she'd eaten at the night before with Lu and Eleanor. She picked a booth in the back, ordered a hamburger and iced tea, and took the binder out of her bag. It held about thirty typed pages double-spaced, with footnotes at the bottom of each. She started reading, taking a break for her hamburger, though she wasn't fully convinced by the researcher's argument, which posited that Ichabod had actually been an American spy who had come to Sleepy Hollow to assess the amount of Loyalist sentiment in the area. Though she didn't fully buy it, Abby got caught up in the idea and she barely noticed the server take her plate.

"So? Was I right about Johanna?"

Abby looked up, startled. Katie stood next to her table, smiling. She had a great smile. The kind that made you want to find out more about her and invite her to dinner. She wore a faded gray sweatshirt that said "Vermont" across the chest and a blue baseball cap that looked like it was probably a favorite of hers. Abby tried to ignore the little current that danced down her thighs, but it didn't work.

"I think there is definitely a case to be made with regard to Katrina's cousin's proclivities," Abby said. "But what about Ichabod? What did Katrina find out about him?"

"You finished box five."

"Yeah. Do I find out in box six?"

"Not that I could tell."

Abby gestured for her to sit across from her and Katie slid into the booth. "So we don't find out what this big secret was?" Abby asked. That was a major historical bummer.

"No. And I tried to track it down in the other boxes." Katie pointed at the binder. "What do you think about that?"

"It's as good a story as any. I hadn't considered the Ichabod-as-war-veteran angle, but it doesn't really explain why he disappeared. I mean, why would the family of a

British loyalist still be pissed off, over a decade after the war, at a spy like Ichabod Crane?"

The server returned and Katie ordered a beer from him. "Do you want anything else?" Katie asked Abby.

"No, I'm good. "

The server left and Katie settled herself more into the booth. Abby tried not to think about the thrill she got when Katie's foot accidentally bumped hers.

"But it's an interesting take, don't you think?" Katie said. "And people carry grudges for a long time. If your family got screwed over in the Revolutionary War and the spy who did most of the screwing suddenly shows up in your neighborhood years later, you might want to do a little ass-kicking. And if the guy dies, oh, well."

"But what's the deal with the horseman? The legend says that the horseman might have been responsible for Ichabod's disappearance."

Katie shrugged. "The horseman at that time could've been a local guy messing with Ichabod. I'd guess Brom Bones, since he was trying to hook up with Katrina. And in the letters, it seems Katrina was leaning toward Ichabod. So Brom thought he'd scare him away. There might have been an accident that Brom didn't count on. The horseman was already a legend, after all, before Ichabod showed up."

Abby sat back, thinking. Katrina had said that Ichabod wasn't who he seemed to be. The spy angle, thus, could answer that question. He was a spy and not a schoolteacher. But why would that both elate and distress Katrina?

"Were the Van Tassels British loyalists?" Abby asked.

"No. At least there's nothing to suggest they were hardcore into that. Though it would make sense if they were because merchant types did tend to stay loyal to the crown. I think they rather enjoyed the prospects of an independent America, but for the most part, it seems they stayed neutral or leaned slightly American." Katie looked up as the server dropped her beer off. "Thanks," she said as he moved away and Abby stared at her profile for a little longer than was necessary.

Katie took a drink, set the glass down and said, "There's no mention in any history in these parts that suggests that about the Van Tassels, though again, there might have been a few in the family tree. But that's a good point, if Ichabod was an American spy who pissed off a local family."

"What about the Van Brunts?"

"Same. From what local history tells us, most of the people in this area were either pro-American or tried to stay neutral. There were some loyalist factions in surrounding communities, and probably a few loyalists in every family, which no doubt created drama at gatherings."

Abby closed the binder. "Are you sure you want to do political science?"

Katie laughed. "I sound like Lu, don't I?"

"A little."

"I'm doing history as a minor field. But I keep my options open. I might change my mind." She took another sip of beer. "Lu says you're working on your dissertation."

"Yes. A community study. I'm interested in how folklore intertwines with local histories and how they influence each other. And that sounded really nerdy, didn't it?"

Katie grinned. "Totally. But I like nerds. A lot."

Abby didn't give herself time to contemplate Katie's statement further because something occurred to her. "Did Johanna leave a journal?"

"Not that I've seen. It's not here, anyway. Why?"

"Because maybe she wrote down the secret that Katrina wanted to tell her about Ichabod."

Katie leaned forward, eyes sparking with excitement. "Duh. Let me ask Lu." She took her phone out and started texting.

"Something that both elated and distressed Katrina," Abby said as Katie texted. "What would make you both excited and bummed at the same time?"

"Flirting with someone who flirts back but then you find out that person is married or partnered." Katie's gaze was still on her phone.

"So maybe Ichabod was married?" That thought hadn't occurred to Abby. And it wasn't in any of the family legends. "But that doesn't make sense. Katrina wouldn't have been elated at finding that out. Bummed, yes. But not elated." And then it dawned on her that Katie had used the word "partnered" along with married. She glanced at Katie's hands. On her right middle finger Katie wore a silver ring with a design carved on it. Abby couldn't tell what it was, but the ring wasn't on the ring finger, so she wasn't married. But she might have a partner. Abby hoped not, and she hoped that Katie preferred women. But then, what good would that do her, since she was only in town for a few more days?

Regardless, Katie was fun to talk to and clearly enjoyed history, though it was a little weird, how easy it was to connect with her about this topic. That didn't happen often, Abby had discovered. It took a certain type to geek out over history. But here they were, talking like they'd known each other for years, and it was a little disconcerting. But Abby liked it. More than she probably should.

"Lu says there's no journal like that here," Katie said, "but it might've ended up in a collection in New York City or with another archive. She said she's going to see what she can find out."

"Excellent. I'm guessing the historical society doesn't have any journals that Katrina kept."

"No. Not that we know of."

"Okay, so I say we rule out the married or partnered thing with regard to Ichabod. Because even if they were flirting, and Katrina found out that Ichabod was married, she wouldn't have been elated. Distressed, maybe, but not happy about it, even if she enjoyed the flirting when it happened."

Katie put her phone down on the table. "Here's what we know. Ichabod was a feminist—as much as he could be back then—he was handsome, and treated Katrina with respect. Plus, she liked him."

"Not just 'liked.' She seemed to be into him," Abby clarified. "And I just don't think finding out that he was a spy is something that would distress her or elate her. So I'm ruling that out, too."

Katie took another sip of beer. "I'm thinking that Katrina and Ichabod had a lot going on, Brom found out, dressed up as the horseman, and basically ran him out of town."

"But that still doesn't explain the secret. God, history can be so damn frustrating."

Katie grinned. "Have you been to the glen?"

"No."

"Want to go? I'll drive. It's only a couple of miles."

"It's dark out."

"That's the best time to go. You'll get a feel for it. And this time of year, lots of people go to ghost watch. So it's not as creepy, I guess, as it could be."

She should probably say no. But Katie's smile and the look in her eyes convinced Abby otherwise. "Okay."

Katie waved the server over and Abby handed him a credit card. Katie gave him cash before Abby could offer to buy the beer.

"Let me ring this up. Be right back," he said to Abby. To Katie, he said, "Do you want change?"

"No." Katie smiled at him then looked at Abby. "Are you staying for the Halloween festivities on Saturday?"

"You're kidding, right? I geek out over folklore. How could I miss something like that?" It was the day after tomorrow. She hoped to get as much research in as possible before then.

Katie smiled and leaned back against the booth. She put her arm up so it lay along the top of it and Abby wondered why a motion that simple could be so enticing. But on Katie, it was. It had been a while since Abby had dated. She had been busy with research and hadn't met anyone lately, so she had quit thinking about it. Until now. Funny how that happened.

"The glen is usually crowded around this time because everybody wants to see the ghost horseman," Katie was saying. "Legend has it this is the best time of the year for sightings. The day of the ride, I know a few places that aren't as packed and generally, our horseman rides there, too. He tries to make a big circuit, so most everybody gets a chance to see him."

"Sounds great," Abby said as the server returned with her card and receipts. She signed and gathered her things to go.

Katie slid out of the booth and Abby followed her, trying to keep her gaze above Katie's waist. She didn't succeed.

She followed Katie to her vehicle, a gray SUV parked right in front and it dawned on Abby that this was the car she'd seen the evening before outside the historical society, and Katie must've been the driver who waved at Lu. Katie unlocked it with her key fob and went around to the driver's side.

"So how'd you know I was at the pub?" Abby asked as she got in and buckled up.

"I didn't. Guess I got lucky." Katie flashed her another smile, put the SUV in reverse and backed out. The interior smelled faintly of vanilla. It had the comfortable, lived-in look of a vehicle that got a lot of use but was well cared for.

"Guess I did, too. After all, I'm getting a ride to the glen."

"Totally my pleasure. Besides, the glen should be part of your research. That's where Ichabod disappeared. Or so they say." Katie accelerated as they hit the edge of town. "It hasn't changed much out here. Some clearing on the edges of the main glen for houses, but other than that, the heart of it has been left pretty much alone for pedestrian traffic. The historical commission in town likes to preserve it, since it's a great tourist attraction."

"Has anybody thought to keep the horseman working year-round?"

"You mean as a regular attraction?"

"Yeah. Or even just a sometime and unpredictable attraction. Just randomly have someone ride around out here and drum up sightings and interest."

"I think there was some discussion about that when I was in high school, but locals decided that was too much crazy for one haunted glen."

Abby laughed.

"Ah. So you're not always a serious scholar." Katie's voice was warm and layered, like a caress.

Another round of sparks zipped through Abby's chest and stomach. Kind of embarrassing, to have a crush on someone she'd just met. "No, not always," Abby said, and to her ears it sounded kind of prudish. "After all, I'm going out to run around in said haunted glen. At night."

"Good point. I stand corrected."

"So what topic are you working on?"

"Just finished my master's last year. I'm actually looking for a topic for a dissertation. I'm interested in early feminist movements, and how those translated in local politics."

"Then your history background serves you really well. Define early."

"Eighteenth and nineteenth centuries, before 1850. I'd like to compare the political campaigns that women were involved in then with some of the more recent ones. Late twentieth century and early twenty-first." She slowed down and turned right. "Because as we know, women were involved in politics, though they couldn't vote."

"True." And Abby thought it was sexy, talking shop with Katie. That made her an even bigger geek, she supposed, but she didn't care.

The SUV lurched a little on what was clearly a dirt road and Katie slowed down. "They do minimal maintenance out here. Local flavor and all." Katie steered first left then right.

"How long has this road been here?" Abby hung onto the grab bar above the passenger window.

"As long as I can remember. I think it's part of the original road through the glen. Lu will probably know." She slowed down and pulled off to the right.

From the headlights, Abby saw thick forest lining either side of the road. Four other cars were parked there. Three were empty. The windows of the fourth were fogged up. Teenagers, no doubt. The area was probably a favorite make-out spot. And most likely, over the years, it had always been one.

The thought of making out made her flush because Katie was the person who popped into her head. "So is there actually a bridge?" Abby asked, since she wanted to stop thinking about kissing Katie.

"There was. Not out here, though. The one described in Irving's story isn't there anymore. But we can check out the replica in the cemetery. And there's some scary but cool stuff that goes on there, too."

"Great."

Katie turned off the engine and looked at Abby. "Do you believe in ghosts?"

"I don't know. There are inexplicable things in the world," Abby said. "And people have been recording sightings and strange phenomena for centuries, so I think there could be something to the idea."

"Most of the stuff people report in the glen is weird lights, weird sounds, and the horseman." Katie took a mini flashlight out of the glove box, reaching across Abby to do so, which brought her very close.

Abby froze. She caught a whiff of Katie's cologne. Crisp and subtle. Abby couldn't put her finger on what the notes were, but she liked it. Katie straightened, turned the vehicle's lights off, and got out. Without the car lights on, Abby realized how very dark this part of the world was. Not much light pollution, either, but if she looked back the way they had come, she could make out a faint glow from the town, hovering over the trees. She got out and shut the door and Katie locked the vehicle.

"If you get freaked out, we'll come back, no problem," Katie said. She turned on her flashlight and started walking up the road. "I'm pretty sure that a lot of the lights that people see up here are ghost hunter flashlights. Especially this time of year." Her own flashlight's narrow beam seemed to stab the hard-packed earth of the road underfoot.

Abby followed, glad she had her keychain flashlight with her. Just in case. "Do *you* believe in ghosts?" She matched her pace to Katie's, which was more like a stroll, fortunately, because the road's surface wasn't completely smooth, and Katie's flashlight didn't pick up some of the potholes right away.

"I take the position you do. I've seen some strange things around here, but so much of it might be influenced by local lore that it could, in turn, be influencing me to see things that I otherwise wouldn't. There. Just laid some psychology on you."

"That's something I think about, in terms of deconstructing folklore and its surrounding cultures. I mean, where do you draw a line between what's history and what's been spun into folklore? How much of a community's culture is influenced by either?"

"I think both are useful for telling stories. And I can tell you really love this topic," Katie added with a soft laugh.

"Yeah. Sorry about that. My inner geek."

"Which I totally enjoy. Don't apologize for it. And stop here."

Abby felt Katie's hand on her arm, gently pulling.

"This is a good spot to see the sky and into the heart of the glen, through the trees. You'll no doubt see some ghost hunters in there, too, but who knows? Maybe there'll be something else." She turned her flashlight off.

They stood in the road and in the light of the rising moon, some of the trees on either side seemed to shift and move, like gnarled and twisted dancers. The hair on the back of Abby's neck stood up. "Okay, I get why people think they see weird things out here."

"Right? Your brain and your eyes mess with you, especially in light like this. Power of suggestion. Look through there—" Katie had her hand on Abby's arm again. "Do you see anything?"

She kept her hand on Abby's arm and Abby was sure the heat from Katie's palm was searing her skin, even through her fleece. Flustered, she tried to focus on whatever Katie might be trying to get her to see. A flash of light between the trees made her stiffen. "I'm going to assume that's a flashlight," she said, trying to sound braver than she felt.

"Probably. Hold on. Keep watching."

The light flickered again, as if it was traveling between trees. A male voice floated in the night air, followed by laughter. Abby exhaled. "Flashlight."

"Shh. Listen for a bit."

Abby tried, but Katie's hand was still on her arm and she suddenly wanted to grab her and pull her close.

"Do you hear anything?" Katie asked.

"You mean besides guys in the woods?"

"Yeah."

Abby maintained silence between them for what seemed like a long time, concentrating so hard on her hearing that she eventually thought she heard her heart pounding in her ears. Maybe that was what people heard when they thought it was the horseman. It wasn't hooves. It was their own fear, pounding in their ears from their heartbeats. Katie took her hand off Abby's arm and the spot, where it had been, cooled abruptly, much to Abby's disappointment.

"Too bad. Guess all you get is guys in the woods tonight," Katie said, and she turned her flashlight back on.

"Well, there's always Saturday."

"You want some company on your folklore quest during the festivities?"

"Depends. Whose?" she teased, seeing what she could get away with.

Katie chuckled and Abby caught the flash of her teeth in the gloom. "Mine. I can drive again, but it's best to leave cars outside the glen, so the horseman has room to maneuver and—"

"It's a deal," Abby said, and then she silently kicked herself for sounding overeager. On the other hand, so what? So, she thought Katie was interesting. And okay, really attractive. There was nothing wrong with spending time with an attractive woman on a research trip. Especially one who knew the collections like Katie did. Logical, right? Abby unsuccessfully tried to convince herself that her interest was purely pragmatic

"Come on," Katie said. "There's an old path up ahead that jags off this road. Whoever the horseman is on Saturday will use it. They always do. Some of the better ones have even ridden through the woods. When they do that, they burst out of the forest and scare the hell out of people walking around out here."

"So he rides his horse through the trees? What about injuries?"

"Like I said, only the better ones do it. One of the best was three years ago and I'm pretty sure it was a woman."

"There are women who ride as the horseman?" Abby moved a little closer to Katie and hoped it wasn't obvious.

"Can't say for sure, since nobody ever knows who the horsemen are year to year, but from what I've heard, there are a few over the years who've been women. Doesn't matter, because it's all about the illusion, after all." Her arm brushed Abby's but before Abby could move away to protect her hormones, Katie stopped.

"That's the path, there to the left."

Here, the trees seemed even closer to the road, branches entwined overhead, blocking the moonlight.

"Do you want to walk a little farther?" Katie asked.

"I think I hear something." Abby stood, straining to pick up the sound she thought she heard over the sighing of the breeze and the creak of wood as tree branches rubbed across each other. Something rhythmic, like hoofbeats. And then it was louder, and Katie gripped Abby's arm and pulled her closer as a figure appeared out of the darkness. And then another. Abby sagged against Katie when she realized there wasn't a horse, just two guys running, their flashlight beams jerking like light sabers with their motions.

"Shit," one guy said when he noticed Abby and Katie.

"What happened?" Abby asked and the guys stopped, breathing hard. In the glows from their flashlights Abby determined them to be high school age.

"Dude without a head," one finally managed. "No horse. Just the dude."

The other guy concurred and then Abby heard laughter and two more guys emerged from the forest, also with flashlights.

"You pussies," one newcomer said to the first two guys. "Got you good." Then he noticed Abby and Katie. "Hey," he said hastily. "Careful out here, ladies. There's a guy without a head." His friend pulled his dark sweatshirt up over his head and walked around, moaning and waving his arms. Katie laughed and Abby, adrenaline spent, laughed, too.

"Assholes," one of the guys who had been running muttered.

"Beware the legend," said sweatshirt dude as they headed back down the road to where Katie had parked.

"Hey," one called back. "You okay? Want to walk with us?"

"No, we're good," Katie answered. "Thanks."

"Beware the legend," the one guy yelled again, and Abby heard them all laugh.

"They're not from around here," Katie said, and at that moment, Abby realized that she was still leaning back against Katie, and that Katie had one arm around Abby's waist.

"How do you know?" Abby tried to figure out how to extricate herself without making it obvious. But she also didn't want to, and she wasn't sure how to do *that* without making it obvious.

"I didn't recognize them." And Katie's breath brushed Abby's ear, sending a jolt of electricity along Abby's nerves from her head to her thighs. She pushed away to hide the shudder of delight that rocketed through her, though she immediately missed the feel of Katie against her.

"Okay. Well. That was exciting," Abby said.

"Completely."

Flustered, Abby started walking back toward the car, thinking it was probably a bad idea to make a pass at a woman she barely knew, in a dark, creepy, and possibly haunted forest. But it was also kind of arousing. She swallowed and quickened her pace a little.

"So," Katie said behind her. "How come you don't go by Tabitha?"

She slowed down, glad for the change in subject. "Too hard to shorten."

"Tab is cute."

"But people tend to draw it out and make it Tabby, which I'm not a fan of. No offense to cats."

Katie laughed. "You don't need to shorten it, actually. It's a pretty name." Her arm brushed Abby's, and Abby moved away just a little, willing herself not to succumb to her attraction, which was entirely too weird, since she'd just officially met Katie that morning.

"What about Katie? Is it short for something?"

"Do you think it is?"

Katie's flashlight revealed her SUV, the only car remaining near the road.

Abby relaxed. "Yes."

"You're right. Care to take a guess?"

"You don't strike me as a Katherine," Abby said as she went around to the passenger side.

"Good. Because I'm not." Katie unlocked the vehicle with her key fob, and Abby got into the passenger side. She was buckled up before Katie had settled herself, and Abby relaxed even more. The seatbelt felt like a barrier between them, and right now, she needed it.

"You're not really a Kaitlyn, either."

"Huh. That one's not too bad." Katie started the engine and backed onto the road. She expertly maneuvered the vehicle around.

"If there were a history of Russians in this area, I might guess Katiana." She could see Katie as a Katya or Katiana.

"Now there's one I like," Katie said as she accelerated. "But no, neither side of my family is overtly Russian. There might've been a Russian or two somewhere in the family tree during the fur-trapping era, but they haven't made it obvious. You're close, though."

Not close enough, Abby thought, and she bit her lip to keep from saying that aloud. "Okay, how about—" she stopped as it dawned on her. "Katrina?"

"Nailed it."

"Seriously?"

"Mmm hmm. And yes, I'm named for Katrina van Tassel. That's my mom's side of the family. And before you say it, I guess it is sort of strange, a Crane and a Van Tassel hanging out a couple hundred years after the fact. Though my last name is McClaren."

Abby filed that information away. "I was actually going to say that it's kind of cool. I mean, what are the odds?" The thought that a descendant of Katrina van Tassel was helping a descendant of Ichabod Crane uncover family history added another layer of weird to the night, but it felt somehow right, like this was how things were supposed to be.

"Fairly high, if you think about it. There are a lot of Van Tassels around here."

"But not many Cranes. Maybe not any besides me. Not like we make it a habit to come to Sleepy Hollow."

Katie turned onto the paved road and sped up. "Well, you should."

"And have some crazy Hessian ghost run us out of town again?" She paused. "Maybe he thought Ichabod was spying for the British and it pissed him off." Abby stole a glance at

44

Katie and wondered what it would be like to reach over and take her baseball cap off then lean in and—

"Maybe Ichabod was a double agent," Katie said. "Spying for America but acting like he was spying for the British. That would throw any Hessian off, dead or otherwise."

Abby laughed.

"You should really do that more," Katie said.

"What?"

"Laugh. It looks really good on you."

Abby gripped the handle of the door hard enough to make her hand go numb. "Clearly, you don't hang out with me enough to realize that I do, in fact, laugh quite a bit."

"I'll definitely work on that," Katie said as she slowed down at the edge of town. She turned onto Main Street, and Abby hoped she meant what she said.

Katie pulled up in front of the bed and breakfast and took her cell out of her back pocket. "What's your phone number?"

Abby gave it to her and Katie entered it. "Texting you now." She finished and looked up, her gaze locking onto Abby's, whose phone chimed in the pocket of her fleece with Katie's text. "Thanks for a great ghost hunt," Katie said. "If I don't see you tomorrow, I'll definitely see you Saturday."

"What time?"

"Festivities really get going around seven. We can go to the glen earlier if you want, but seven usually works. Or we can go downtown at six and get something to eat. There're usually all kinds of vendors."

"That'll work."

"See you then. Right here." She motioned at the front of the bed and breakfast.

"Okay. Thanks for the ride and the company." Abby unbuckled her seat belt and got out because she knew if she hesitated, she'd do something she wasn't sure about. As good as she imagined it would feel kissing Katie, it was probably a bad idea. She grabbed her bag off the floor of the SUV and closed the door. Katie waited until she had unlocked the main door of the bed and breakfast and then she pulled away, and Abby leaned against the wall just inside for a few moments, wondering what exactly it was about Katie that had her all out of sorts. She took that thought to bed.

Lore

DARK. AS DARK AS THE inside of a cave. Somewhere she heard a beating heart. Was it hers? She strained, listening. Not her heart. Something else. Getting closer. A pounding on hard soil. The darkness decreased and her surroundings took shape into a forest whose trees seemed to move closer together, as if preventing her from slipping between them.

She felt the pounding now, through the soles of her feet on the packed soil beneath them. She couldn't run, she couldn't hide. She was frozen, heartbeat matching the approaching hoofbeats. At that speed, she'd be run down. She tried to scream, tried to say something—anything—but her voice was frozen, too.

A massive black horse emerged from the darkness as if it had pushed through a heavy curtain, its flanks heaving with its exertions, bit clinking in its teeth. Its rider drew it up short, and they paced in front of her, the horse's eyes seemingly flashing in the gloom, the rider's tack creaking and jingling. The rider had no head.

Abby's bones ached from trying to run. The rider eased the horse forward, toward her, and she couldn't even collapse. The horse snorted and its huge head came so close that its breath blew her hair back from her face and she smelled something dank, like mildew on ancient rock. The rider wheeled the horse *around and drew a sword, which he pointed first at Abby and then he held it high, like a salute, and the horse reared onto its back legs, the rider and his sword a vertical line to the ground. And then the horse turned and galloped back the way it had come, hoofbeats thrumming up through Abby's shoes until they faded and she was falling—*

She lurched awake, bathed in sweat and breathing like she'd been running. She lay still in bed for a few minutes. It might've been a bad idea to go to the glen and get all freaked out, Katie notwithstanding. She glanced at the bedside clock radio. Just past one. Too late to text anyone. Weird, what the brain could manufacture.

Abby got out of bed and went to the window. Her room overlooked Main Street. To her left was the heart of downtown, a couple of blocks away. The streetlights cast pools of light onto the street and sidewalk, but nothing besides fallen leaves moved in the street or across the lawns of the nearby houses, historic cottages nestled between a few multi-story New England saltbox-style homes. She opened the window and listened for a bit, ignoring the cold. The rustle of dead leaves in the breeze, scraping against cement as they blew across sidewalks. A dog in the distance. No pounding hoofbeats. No headless rider careening down the street on a huge black horse. She closed the window, relieved, and got back into bed.

Her tablet sat on the nightstand next to the clock and she turned it on. Halfway through the comedy she'd selected to stream, she was sufficiently relaxed to go back to sleep and her last thoughts were of Katie's smile.

"Does anybody ever report seeing Katrina van Tassel's ghost?" Abby asked Lu the next morning over coffee in the historical society break room. She'd had eggs and fruit at the bed and breakfast already, but she could always do with more coffee. And maybe a donut.

"Yes, actually. Sometimes there's mention of a woman dressed in what reports call 'an old-fashioned dress' in the glen. Other reports have her at the pub, which used to be the Van Tassel family home."

"What did she look like?"

"There's a portrait of her in the pub, above the bar. Did you see it?"

"No." She'd have to work on her powers of observation.

"Well, it's based on a painting we have in the vault. Come on."

Deciding it was better to focus on Katrina than to let her nightmares distract her, Abby left her coffee on the break room table and followed Lu downstairs.

"We keep it protected," Lu said as she unlocked one of the flat metal drawers that looked like it might've been used to store maps. "It's in a climate controlled environment." She slid the drawer open, and beneath what looked like plexiglass was an oil painting in an ornate wooden frame of a woman from the torso up. She wore a white dress, cut in such a way to show off a bit of her shoulders and neck. She looked straight out at the viewer, an enigmatic little smile playing at the corners of her mouth. Her reddish-blond hair had been swept up and her eyes—hazel, Abby decided—seemed to spark with mischief.

"Wow. She was beautiful. And the artist was really good."

Lu laughed. "Is it any wonder Ichabod may have been interested?" She shut the drawer and locked it, and Abby followed her back upstairs.

"Do you think that was true?" Abby asked.

Lu chose another donut from the box. "That Ichabod and Brom Bones vied for Katrina's attentions?" She asked before taking a bite.

"Yes."

"The legends suggest that. And Katrina's correspondence with Johanna certainly indicated that she had more than a passing interest in Ichabod. You'll find more of those references in box six. She also wrote rather disparaging things about Brom."

"Yeah, I've come across some of those." Abby poured herself another cup of coffee from the pot on the sink counter. "Katrina thought Ichabod was handsome. And from her description, he doesn't sound anything like what the popular legends say about him."

"That's not unusual. From Katrina's correspondence, Ichabod was somewhat of a social rebel. So the legend formed to create the narrative that presented him as an awkward and superstitious man, thus justifying whatever happened to him."

Abby nodded. She'd seen that many times in historical records. She liked that Ichabod was sort of a rebel, and that he may have had a romance with Katrina van Tassel. She ate another donut and finished her coffee. Being here helped her dream from the night before fade even more. Ten minutes later she was settled in the reading room with box six.

By the third file, she was thoroughly engrossed in Katrina's letters. Some she re-read because she got caught up in Katrina's stories. It was cool how you could get a sense of someone from the letters they wrote. Katrina had different personas with different people in her circle of friends and family. She was sly, witty, and maybe a little outrageous in her turns of phrase when she wrote to Johanna. But to older relatives or non-family associates, she was formal and, in some cases, demure. Abby liked how Katrina would sometimes slip a little rebelliousness into those letters, though, like when she mentioned local politics that favored women. Katrina would have made an excellent politician, Abby thought as she read. She knew exactly what to say and how to say it, depending on the audience.

At one point Abby checked the clock and stretched. Two hours had passed and she hadn't even noticed, she had been so caught up in Katrina's world and the glimpses of late eighteenth-century America revealed through her flowing script. She was a little over halfway through this box, but she didn't mind diving right back in.

She didn't hear the door open and when Katie spoke, it made her jump.

"Hey," Katie said. "Sorry to bother you."

"No, it's okay." And it was. It was more than okay.

"I mean, I didn't want to tear you away from your work, but we've got a couple of pizzas out here. Want some?"

Abby glanced at the clock. It was nearly one. "Sure."

Katie held the door for her and as Abby passed, she wondered why Katie had to look so good in jeans. These were low slung, and she'd accessorized with a wide leather belt. She wore a plain denim shirt tucked into her jeans. No baseball cap today. Her hair was pulled back into a ponytail again, and it left her neck exposed and oh, how Abby wanted to kiss it. She contented herself watching Katie walk.

Robert and Eleanor were in the break room munching on pizza, so Abby couldn't chat with Katie one-on-one, which was a little disappointing, but at least she was able to be near her. On the plus side, Katie followed her back to the reading room.

"How far along are you in that box?" she asked as they entered.

"Almost done. And seriously, Katrina had the hots for Ichabod."

Katie laughed. "Right? I was waiting for you to get that far. I think they had a rendezvous," she said, putting salacious emphasis on "rendezvous."

"I totally see that. I'm almost up to when he disappeared, at least according to legend."

Katie took the chair next to her. "I don't think Ichabod died that night."

Abby looked over at her. "I don't, either. I mean, I don't have proof, but it doesn't feel right."

"So what happened to him?"

Abby put her gloves back on and returned a folder to the box. "If Katrina and Ichabod were having an affair, maybe somebody found out about it. Ichabod had some ideas that weren't too popular with a lot of people then, and maybe it was a bad idea for them to be seeing each other. After all, Baltus wanted Katrina to marry Brom."

"So if he didn't die, what happened?"

Abby pulled the next folder. "I think he either got run out of town or Katrina asked him to leave to protect himself."

"I like that. A romance for the ages. Maybe Ichabod escaped and he and Katrina carried on an affair for years. Maybe they even had kids. Which means you might have some relatives out there that you didn't even know about."

"Cranes galore," Abby said with a grin.

Katie smiled. She pushed back from the table and stood. "I'll let you get back to work. Just wanted to see how you're doing. Catch you later. For sure tomorrow."

"Definitely." Abby watched her leave, trying not to be obvious, but Katie threw her a look from the other side of the glass door that made her insides feel like she was on a rollercoaster. As delicious as this crush was, it was also confusing. She didn't know if Katie was single. And she wasn't going to ask, since she was only here another few days and starting anything with someone would invariably lead to complications and long-distance crap.

Unless Katie was just into a fling. Abby opened the file and stared at the first page without seeing it. Could she herself do a fling? Katie was attractive. Funny. Interesting. Could Abby have a crazy passionate affair with someone she'd just met? Women like Katie definitely made her consider that option, though she preferred something a little slower, with a super hot buildup. She focused on the open file. Consider that later, she remonstrated herself. She was here to gather information and materials for her dissertation.

An hour later, she came upon a letter from Katrina to Johanna that mentioned Ichabod's disappearance, dated mid-November, 1799. "My dear Mr. Crane has not been seen for several days. Brom reports that the horseman appeared the night Mr. Crane was last seen, and frightened him so badly that he ran and may have become lost in the forest. I know better. And I shall tell you about it the next time I see you, though I'm sure you have guessed, as well, what happened."

Abby read through the rest of the letters. "What happened?" she asked the silent files. "Come *on*, Katrina. Don't leave me hanging like this." Dammit. History mystery, and she was so close. So damn close to finding something out about Ichabod. She took box six back to Lu and switched it out with box seven and started immediately reading to see if Katrina mentioned anything else about Ichabod. Almost through the box and into the year 1800, she hadn't mentioned him at all.

"What the hell?" Abby muttered. A guy Katrina clearly had something with disappears and that's it? No further mentions? She went back through, starting with the end of 1799 and going through the summer of 1800. No mention of Ichabod.

"That's cold," Abby said to the box. Katrina had let Johanna, especially, believe that Ichabod meant something to her and then she totally dropped him from her vocabulary after he disappeared. She felt an odd protectiveness for Ichabod, two hundred years after the fact. "She burned you," she said to him. She knew what that was like, so she sympathized with him. Even if he had died on that night, and not known that Katrina hadn't been that into him, Abby still felt bad for him.

"How are things going?" Lu stood at the door, holding it open. Abby hadn't noticed her approach.

"He really did disappear. Not just in legend, but from the historical record."

"Well, from these records, anyway."

"It doesn't make sense." Abby leaned back in her chair. "Why would you not mention someone you had feelings for after he disappears? All her correspondence to Johanna up to that point indicates that she really liked him. And then he disappears and…nothing."

Lu offered a wan smile. "Perhaps she was grieving. Sometimes that's how people cope. Especially then, before counseling. People did what they had to do to deal with tragedy."

Abby considered that, but it didn't feel right. Katrina had shared quite a bit with Johanna and some of her other relatives and friends. Not mentioning Ichabod after his disappearance seemed out of character for her. "Maybe those letters to Johanna are missing," Abby said. "Where she mentioned him after he disappeared."

"That's possible, but this is one of the most—if not *the* most—complete collections of the Van Tassel family's materials, and I don't know of any other letters to Johanna in any other collection. Which reminds me, I'm still trying to find out if there's a journal that Johanna left that perhaps we missed. I'll let you know."

"Thanks. But seriously, it seems so sad, to just stop talking about him like that."

"We do take history personally," Lu said with a chuckle. "Since you've read into 1800, I presume you've come across Elizabeth in Katrina's letters."

"Yeah."

"She's another mystery. Katrina never refers to a last name for her, so we don't know who she was. But they do seem to share a bond of sorts. At any rate, we'll be closing in an hour."

Abby nodded. "Okay. Thanks for the heads-up. I seem to lose track of time in here."

"Contemporary time."

Abby laughed. "Good point."

Lu smiled and left and Abby sat for a moment, thinking. She hadn't really paid attention to Elizabeth. Maybe she should. She started reading again, from the days after Ichabod disappeared and found what appeared to be Elizabeth's first appearance in December, in a letter Katrina wrote to Johanna. "My dear friend Elizabeth shall be accompanying me to New York next month, and I'm sure you will find her company enjoyable, though certainly not as enjoyable as I. You know a bit about the story of our meeting—"

Wait. What? Abby went back through the letters. Had she missed mention of that? No, she hadn't. No mention of it. But in November of 1799, Katrina said she would be visiting New York for Christmas. She must've told Johanna about Elizabeth in person over the holiday. She deliberately said nothing about her until she was in New York, physically in the presence of Johanna. Abby frowned. Which meant she didn't want to mention anything about her in a letter.

"Why the hell didn't you keep a journal?" Abby asked the letter. She continued reading, this time much more carefully with regard to Elizabeth, and by the time she'd gotten through box seven, she was convinced that the mysterious Elizabeth was, in fact, another target of Katrina's ardor. "She is handsome, for a woman," Katrina wrote in March 1800. "Of that sort of beauty one is drawn to whether the bearer is male or female. And, dear Johanna, she is utterly devoted to education, especially for those less privileged. I feel a continued connection with her, and long for each time I see her, and hear her laugh. She will be here in two days' time. I can scarcely wait."

Okay, this was an interesting turn of events. Katrina dumped (or got over really quickly) Ichabod for a woman. Abby checked the clock. Damn. Time to go. She carefully packed up box seven just as Lu appeared.

"And what have you decided about Elizabeth?" Lu asked as she checked the box and Abby's laptop bag.

"I think Katrina was in love with her."

"That's what Katie and I think. Robert is less convinced, using the old 'language and times were different then' argument to suggest they were just good friends. Eleanor goes back and forth between my argument and Robert's."

"It seems that Elizabeth returned her affections, at least from the letters included here. Are there letters between Katrina and Elizabeth?"

"Unfortunately, no. Not that we know of."

"What happened to her?"

"Oh, you'll find mention of her throughout the next few years. Katrina, sadly, died about ten years after Ichabod disappeared. Elizabeth is present in Katrina's letters until the end."

Abby slung her bag over her shoulder. "Did Katrina have kids?"

"She ended up marrying Brom Bones in 1803."

Abby groaned. "So that part of the legend is true."

Lu grinned. "Family pressures. Women—even those of means—didn't have many options then. Regardless, it appears that she carried on a longstanding relationship of some kind with this Elizabeth, even after that. She had two children, both of whom survived into adulthood and had children of their own. A son and a daughter. He was named Isaac and she was named Elizabeth."

"Why did she die?" Abby followed Lu out of the reading room, wondering if Katrina had named her daughter after the woman she apparently loved.

"An unspecified illness. Not uncommon then."

Abby waited for her at the front counter. "What happened to Katrina's children?" she asked when Lu reappeared.

"Isaac, like many Van Brunts and Van Tassels, became a merchant. He ended up in Boston while Elizabeth married a magistrate in New York. Both had several children who survived into adulthood, a few of whom moved back to Sleepy Hollow and continued farming and running businesses, keeping up traditions with the family holdings." Lu put her jacket on and picked up her backpack. "We have some of those papers here, but many are in Boston, with Isaac's collections. Elizabeth's are in New York City, with the collections of her husband. I'll get more information on those for you." She moved to the door and armed the security system then flipped the sign on the door to "Closed."

Abby followed her outside and waited for her to finish locking up. "It's a fascinating story, but it doesn't tell me what happened to Ichabod."

"Ah," Lu said. "That, my dear, is a matter of conjecture and legend. He disappeared from the historical record as well as from Sleepy Hollow. But I've always wondered, did he really disappear?"

"What do you mean?" Abby walked with Lu toward downtown.

"He may have been the victim of an unfortunate accident and Brom Bones may have been the one to create the circumstances in which that happened. However, this was an even smaller community then. Surely Katrina would've been aware of what Brom was about that night. Why would she marry the man who caused an accident to the man she may have been in love with?"

Abby pondered that. "The legends suggest Brom did cause it but that he kept it secret."

"And secrets can be kept. But Katrina seemed too savvy for that. Brom, to her, was a not-too-bright oaf, so the idea that he could have orchestrated an accident and then kept it secret from her—well, it doesn't ring true."

They walked in silence for a few moments until Abby spoke again. "Katrina wrote about the horseman a few times, so she knew the stories about him. And people might believe that a ghost scared Ichabod to death."

"True," Lu said. "Remember, the legends say nothing about a body. So if Ichabod died that night, his body was never found."

"And the legend served that purpose. No body, no explanation, so why not pin a disappearance on a ghost who already had a prominent position in the folklore of the area?"

Lu stopped. "I have to turn here. And you should really talk to Katie. She's fascinated by the story, too, and has been through the collection a few times. She has a couple of interesting theories. I'll let her tell you. Oh, and don't forget. We close at three tomorrow to get ready for Halloween. Not often that it falls on a Saturday."

"Okay. See you tomorrow."

Lu waved and walked away from Main Street into what was a more residential part of town, Abby knew, because she'd driven around a little the day she arrived. A mixture of New England-style saltbox houses, later bungalow-style, and even a smattering of Queen Annes. Abby pictured Lu in a bungalow.

She continued downtown, on her way to the bed and breakfast when she paused and dug her phone out of her bag. She started to text Katie then stopped. Maybe Katie was busy. It was Friday evening, after all, and already almost nightfall. Maybe she had a girlfriend. That didn't sit well with Abby, but it was something to consider. Though it seemed Katie had been flirting with her since they met... She resumed the text, sent it, and started walking again.

Buildings and businesses were festooned with banners about the festival and the horseman's ride, and practically every business window had Halloween decorations and notices about the ride, too. Abby caught a vibe of anticipation as she walked and overheard bits of conversations about the upcoming festival, and at least one person wondered aloud who was riding as the horseman this year. Damn, she'd meant to ask Lu about how the horseman was chosen.

Her phone rang and she checked the ID, which made her smile. She answered, still walking. "Hey."

"Hey, yourself," Katie said. "So Lu's been telling stories about me again."

"Maybe a little. She said you have some theories about Ichabod's disappearance that you clearly haven't told me yet." Abby tried to convince herself that this was all about research, that she just wanted to talk to Katie again because of their shared interest in history. She tried. And failed, as Katie laughed, low in her ear.

"Don't want to blow all my conversation cred with you at once," she said. "I'm actually at the pub right now, if you want to swing by."

Abby slowed down. The pub was right across the street. "Are you sure? I mean, if you're hanging out with your friends or something, I'll just talk to you tomorrow." Because if she was there with a girlfriend, Abby really didn't want to see that and she really didn't want to meet her. She'd rather just keep her crush to herself and not think about Katie with another woman.

"I actually just stopped by a few minutes ago to chat up the bartender," Katie said. "We went to high school together. Seriously. Come on by."

"Okay. It'll only be a minute. I'm pretty close."

"Excellent. See you in a bit. Bye." Katie hung up and Abby put her phone back in her bag, anticipation zinging up and down her nerves. As crushes went, this one was pretty bad. Still, she liked the way it felt. Most of the time, her crushes didn't go anywhere, but they were fun while they lasted. She crossed the street and went into the pub.

Katie waved her over from the barstool where she sat. "Hi," she greeted Abby. "This is Gary, the most awesome bartender in this part of New York. Maybe in the entire state. Gary, this is Abby. A scholar extraordinaire who just might solve the mystery of Sleepy Hollow."

Abby laughed. "I don't know about that, but it's fun to think about. Nice to meet you."

He grinned and the movement lifted his mustache. "Good to meet you. What can I get you?"

Abby hung her bag on one of the hooks under the bar. Katie was drinking a beer, a beverage Abby didn't like much. "Do you have a cider on tap?"

"Sure do. Coming up." He moved off to take care of the order.

"Put it on my tab," Katie said and Gary nodded.

"Are you sure?" Abby situated herself on the stool next to Katie.

"Yep. So how far did you get today?"

"The end of box seven."

Katie took a sip of her beer. "Good. You've met Elizabeth. But here's my theory about Ichabod."

Gary placed a pint glass of cider on a coaster in front of Abby and a small bowl of bar snacks between them. Mini pretzel sticks and peanuts, mostly.

Katie picked out a couple of pretzel sticks and ate one. "Okay, my theory," she said after she'd finished chewing and swallowing, "and we did talk about this a bit, is that Ichabod didn't die."

"I'm leaning that way, too." Abby sipped the cider. Not too tart, not too sweet. She approved.

"But he wasn't found," Katie continued. "I've wondered why that is. If he was dead, wouldn't someone eventually find his body? It's not like there are deep gorges around here that he'd fall into. So if he had an accident and he was lying unconscious, it stands to reason that he would've been found like that. I mean, like the movie *Sleepy Hollow* with Johnny Depp. Those bodies were found right away."

"That was a movie. Maybe everybody was too scared to go outside to look for him in real life," Abby said.

"I think Katrina would've gone. And guys wouldn't have let her go alone." Katie picked another pretzel stick out of the bowl. "Anyway, his body wasn't found. So, what if he left Sleepy Hollow on purpose? What if he staged the whole thing so he *could* disappear?"

"Why?"

"Any number of reasons. If he was having an affair with Katrina, her dad could've found out and been pissed about it. Brom could've found out and threatened to bail on any intended wedding. Baltus was big into linking the Van Tassels and the Van Brunts." She popped the pretzel stick into her mouth.

Abby nodded, thinking. "However, we know Ichabod had a secret. Whatever it was, he confided in Katrina. Maybe that secret is the key and maybe Katrina helped him disappear. Maybe it doesn't have to do with Brom or Baltus."

"I've thought about that, too. It makes for a great story if nothing else." Katie brushed her hands on her jeans. "Here's another theory. I think Elizabeth was in on whatever plot it was to make him disappear."

"But she doesn't show up until after he was already gone."

"Right. Katrina was sneaky, though. She didn't put anything on paper that she didn't want people finding out. So Elizabeth could've easily been part of the plot from the beginning and Katrina just kept her name out of her letters until after Ichabod was gone. That would protect Elizabeth from any fallout."

Abby took another sip of her cider. "And I guess that would explain why Katrina didn't seem to care about Ichabod after he was gone. Because he really wasn't."

"Exactly," Katie said, a note of triumph in her voice. "Because she knew where he was and they were still in contact. Elizabeth could've been the go-between."

Abby picked a peanut out of the bowl. "But Katrina seemed to have the hots for Elizabeth, too."

"And why not?" Katie pointed at the portrait of her that hung over the bar, above the top shelf liquor. "She was hot herself. And she said in her letters that Elizabeth was attractive."

The dim lighting didn't do Katrina's portrait justice, Abby thought. "Well, there's that."

"Maybe Ichabod went off to sea or something and left Katrina behind. She wasn't one to sit around pining away. So she hooked up with Liz and they carried on even after Katrina married Brom." She grinned. "That could be another great story." She pointed at Abby with a pretzel stick. "Somebody should do a biography of Katrina."

Abby smiled. "Maybe somebody should," she said, using another pretzel stick to point at Katie. "And then there's the legend."

"Katrina totally helped create it," Katie stated, matter-of-fact. "I wonder sometimes if she staged a sighting of the horseman to add to Ichabod's disappearance."

Abby stared at her. "I hadn't thought about that."

"It seems logical, if we go with the idea that Katrina helped Ichabod disappear. She'd want to direct attention away from anybody who might be associated with Ichabod, and what better way to do that than to link his disappearance to a known ghost who happens to like riding around the glen?"

"Did somebody say 'ghost'?"

Abby looked at Gary, who was refilling his bar condiments container. "We're just talking about the legends around here," she replied.

"I've seen him," he said, putting maraschino cherries into one of the container slots. "The horseman."

Abby glanced over at Katie, who was digging through the bowl of snacks. She looked back at Gary. "What did he look like?" she asked him.

"Big black horse. The horseman was decked out in dark colors and he had a sword."

The hair on the back of Abby's neck stood up. "What happened?"

"A bunch of us in high school were running around the glen one night. We were always going down there to scare each other."

Abby looked at Katie again, who gave her a sheepish smile.

"I was waiting behind a tree just off the road that goes through the glen," Gary continued, "because I had the bright idea to jump out from behind it at a couple of my friends."

"You never told me this story," Katie said.

"I thought I did. I told a lot of people, but of course, the thing about legends is that you can believe in them whether you see the ghost or not. Most people figured I'd made it up to add to the legend." He shrugged. "Which is legit, but I know what I saw."

"So what happened?" Abby gripped her glass of cider with both hands.

"I heard this pounding. You know, like they say. Horse's hooves. I stayed behind the tree and swear to God, the horseman rode past. Right past my tree, not six feet away. And then the horse jumped, like there was something in the road, and disappeared. Like the night had swallowed it."

"Dude, seriously?" Katie asked. She held a pretzel stick up like she had intended to eat it but forgot she had it.

"Scared the piss out of me. It was a week before Halloween, so I guess it's possible that someone was out testing the roads. But why would someone go out there in full costume, anyway, before the event? It's a pain in the ass to get all decked out like that."

"Did the horse have red glowing eyes?" Abby asked.

"Not that I remember. Why?"

"Some of the reports of the horseman say the horse has those." Katie ate the pretzel stick she'd been holding. "Other reports don't mention that. But all say the horse is big and black and the rider is always dressed in dark clothes and carries a sword."

"What about the horseman's head?" Abby asked.

Gary looked at her. "Um, he didn't have one."

Katie laughed. "I think she means, was he carrying his head? Or have it on his saddle or something?"

"Oh. No, not that I could tell. But then, I wasn't really looking for it. I just froze, totally scared."

Katie shook her head. "Damn, Gary. That's a hell of a story."

"I didn't go back there for a while. When I did, I didn't see or hear anything after that. So I do wonder sometimes if it was somebody just out joyriding to fuck with people. Power of suggestion and all that. I'm open to being wrong about a ghost, but at the time, I thought it was supernatural." He moved away to talk with a server at the other end of the bar.

"I learn something new every day." Katie picked up her beer.

"Speaking of the horseman," Abby said, "how does he—or she—get chosen to ride for the festival?"

"That's a whole other legend. Lu says the tradition started in the 1980s, and there's a secret society that chooses riders."

"Oh, come on."

"Seriously. With the blessing of the town council. Some local guys started the tradition. Nobody knows how many people are in this group, but it's sort of like a Mardi Gras krewe. I heard you pay dues to help keep the costumes up, but you can't ever talk about it. So nobody outside that group—not even your family—knows you ride."

"Now *that's* a story. First rule of Fight Club—"

"Is you never talk about Fight Club," Katie finished with a smile.

"Anyway, making a legend to buttress another legend that is woven into the history of this town. Wow. Mind blown."

Katie laughed and finished her beer. "I would love to stay and talk to you for a bunch more hours, but I'm having dinner with my folks tonight." She stood and took her jacket off its hook underneath the bar. "You're welcome to come along if you want. My folks like meeting people I hang out with. One of my brothers will be there. The one who claims he's starving all the time."

"That's a nice offer, but maybe next time. I need to write up some notes." The friend zone, Abby thought. That's where Katie had put her. You only took friends home to meet your folks this early in the game. Disappointment sat in her stomach like a bad meal.

"You sure?"

"Yeah. Maybe another time."

"All right." Katie put her jacket on. "We're still on for tomorrow, right?"

"Yes, absolutely." She hoped she didn't sound as bummed as she felt. Well, that's what crushes were about. Getting crushed. Whatever. She could still enjoy Katie's company. And looks. And her laugh and smile, too. Abby forced one of those to her lips.

"Great. I am so looking forward to it." Katie squeezed Abby's forearm and left, but this time, Abby forced herself not to watch her walk away.

"Would you like another cider?"

Abby looked up at Gary, deciding. "Yes. And could I have a menu?"

"Yep. Here you go." He handed her one then filled another pint glass for her.

"Katie said you'd been friends since high school," Abby said as Gary put the glass in front of her and picked up her nearly empty one.

"Yeah, but we've known each other since grade school. I had a tough time in high school. She was really supportive."

"Are you okay now?"

"Oh, yeah. High school's rough on everybody, but more so if you're different."

"High school wasn't good to me, either," Abby said.

"I came out."

She'd picked that vibe up from him. "That must've been hard."

Gary shrugged.

"I waited to do that publicly until after high school," she said, letting him know that she could empathize with what he had gone through.

"Yeah, I probably should have waited. Katie stuck by me, though she took some shit for being gay, too. Eventually, the worst of them left me alone." He smiled again. "Katie's one of those people who can be a total geek and a jock at the same time and she has a huge heart. Huge."

"So are things better for you now?" Life in a small town could be hard on gay people, she knew too well. But she was extremely glad that Katie was indeed gay. Even though she may have been relegated to Katie's friend zone.

"Definitely."

"If it's not too personal, are you, um, seeing anyone? And if you are, do you have to go to a bigger place to visit?"

He grinned. "Yes. And no, because he lives here, too."

"That's good. And that must've sounded weird, asking you that."

"Nah," he said, reassuring. "Are you from a small town?"

"Yes. In Connecticut. But I'm at UConn now."

"Which definitely opens up the dating pool. It did for Katie when she moved away. I just got lucky." He switched out the bowl of snacks with one that was full.

"Oh?" Abby tried not to sound too interested in Katie's dating life.

"Yeah. Binghamton has a much better scene than here. Obviously."

"That makes sense."

"She's not currently seeing anyone that I know of," he said as he poured a beer. "Plus, she's picky. How about you?" He looked over at her.

"I don't really have time to, uh, do that." Katie wasn't currently seeing anyone?

"Why not? There's probably a great scene at UConn."

"Grad school keeps me busy. Not much time." She fiddled with the bar napkin.

"Maybe you should re-think your schedule. Have some fun." He finished with the beer and let it sit under the tap.

"Hmm," she said, noncommittal.

"A cute thing like you would have lots of options," he said with a grin.

"Um." At the moment, there was only one option she'd like to explore.

"Do you know what you'd like?" Gary asked.

Besides Katie? "Veggie burger and fries." She'd probably end up knowing what this restaurant served by heart by the time she went back to Connecticut. Abby handed the menu back, relieved about the change in subject. As Gary went to the cash register, she thought about the night before, when Katie's arm wrapped around her waist in the glen, and her lips had been really close to Abby's ear. That didn't feel like friend zone. Tonight, however, did.

Maybe the atmosphere in the glen had skewed her perceptions and Katie was just being nice. But at least Abby knew Katie was single. So if something *did* happen, there wouldn't be weird drama. But ultimately, why did it matter? She wasn't here for that, after all. She took her tablet out of her bag along with her keyboard. She needed to flesh out her notes while things were still fresh.

Legends

"ICHABOD," SAID A WOMAN'S VOICE *from the forest. "Where are you?"*

Abby struggled once again with movement, worked to take a step but she couldn't. Nor could she cry out.

"Ichabod." A woman emerged from the surrounding trees, wrapped in a dark cloak. "There you are," she said, and she smiled in the moonlight. Katrina?

Abby looked around for Ichabod, but there was no one else in the glen. The woman closed the space between them and her hand cupped Abby's cheek, the touch like fire on her skin. "My love, you must go."

The woman definitely looked like Katrina van Tassel from the painting. "I'm not Ichabod," Abby tried to say but no words came out. And then she felt a familiar vibration beneath her feet, like a drum. "The horseman," she tried to say, but the woman didn't heed her.

"Go," Katrina said. "Before anyone sees."

Abby struggled against the forces that kept her moored to this spot, and finally, with a mighty effort, she managed a step and then another. Katrina had disappeared and finally Abby was able to run and she did, through the forest, dodging trees whose branches seemed to reach for her, creaking and straining to contain her. She heard the pounding all around her, and then she burst out of the forest onto a hard-packed road, where she stumbled but caught herself.

"This way."

Abby whirled toward the voice and froze, confronted by a great black horse a few feet away. The rider on its back was neither headless nor a man. Instead, the woman in the dark cloak gazed down at her. "This way," she said again, and she spurred the horse in the opposite direction and as Abby watched, Katrina's frame morphed into a broad-shouldered headless form that drew a sword before the horse leapt into the air and disappeared, like it had jumped through a rip in the night.

"Go, Ichabod. Before they see."

Katrina stood behind her now. "My love, it's the only way. Hurry."

And Abby started to run, like the horseman was after her, and she plunged back into the forest—

—and snapped awake, sweating and shaking.

"Dammit," she muttered as she sat up in bed. Clearly, she'd allowed herself too much immersion in her subject. And Gary's story at the pub hadn't helped, either. She turned the light on next to the bed and got up to go to the bathroom. Afterward, she looked out the window at the quiet street below. Nothing out of the ordinary. Just like last night.

She got back into bed and again watched a movie on her tablet. By the time it was over, she was able to go back to sleep and this time, she imagined the feel of Katie's arms around her and Katie's lips on her neck.

Like the previous day, Abby made it to the historical society a half-hour before it opened. She called Lu on her cell, and Lu came and opened the door for her.

"Coffee's up. Come on back. It's just me today, though Katie might stop by."

Abby tried to ignore the thrill she got that Katie could stop by later, but she was not successful. If Katie didn't, she'd see her later, which gave her even more thrills. She followed Lu into the break room, where Lu poured her a cup of coffee and motioned at the box of donuts. Abby selected a chocolate one and took a bite before she poured half-and-half into her coffee.

"Katie tells me you two came up with several interesting theories about Ichabod's disappearance."

"Maybe. They're just theories." Small towns, Abby thought. News travels fast.

"But plausible. And if nothing else, they make great fodder for story-telling." Lu bit into a donut and chewed, a thoughtful expression on her face. "I was a little disappointed that neither of my kids got bitten by the history bug. And actually surprised when it was apparent that Katie was the one who enjoyed it as much as I do. Out of all my nieces and nephews, she wasn't the one I figured would be interested."

"Katie's your niece?" Abby stared at her.

Lu smiled. "She doesn't generally tell people right off. Katie tends to be a little private at first. Her mother is one of my sisters."

"So you're a Van Tassel, too."

"Yes, though my last name is different. And yes, local history is also family history for me, which might be why I've grown so fond of it and this place."

"A sense of place is important in every story." Abby finished the donut. "How long has that road been in the glen?"

"You mean the dirt road that takes you through it?"

Abby nodded.

"In its current form, since the 1970s. It was graded over an even older road that wasn't much more than a couple of wagon wheel tracks. Basically, that route through the glen has been in continuous use for decades. Probably centuries." The phone rang from the front counter.

"Be right back. What box do you want?"

"Eight."

"Meet you in the reading room."

Abby finished her coffee and headed to the reading room, where she waited for Lu to bring up the box she'd requested.

"Here you go," Lu said as she placed it on the table. "Remember, we're closing early today."

"Yep. But you'll probably have to remind me again."

Lu laughed and left Abby to the history of Sleepy Hollow.

This time Abby went slowly through the first half of the box, reading through each document carefully. Elizabeth remained a fixture in Katrina's letters to Johanna and sometimes in other letters, but in those, Katrina didn't use the same language. Instead, Elizabeth was a "friend" or "acquaintance." In letters to Johanna, however, Elizabeth was "dear" and, in one instance, "my heart."

"Oh, yeah," Abby said to the document. "You were totally hooking up with Liz." She opened another folder but didn't start reading. Instead, she thought about her dream the night before. The woman in the dream had been Katrina, she was sure, because she resembled the portrait. No surprise, then, that her brain had conjured that image up. But why the hell had the dream Katrina called her Ichabod?

She puzzled over that, even though dreams weren't supposed to make sense. Most likely, because she was a Crane and had been trying to piece together what had happened to her long-dead relative, her brain had simply put her in Ichabod's place in the dream scenario. After all, she didn't have a clear image of what he had looked like. Just snippets of descriptions from Katrina's letters. Plus, she had gotten pretty involved in their history.

It was just the power of suggestion. She started reading through more of Katrina's correspondence to Johanna. Katrina described a recent horseback trip she'd taken to a neighboring village in the summer of 1800. Katrina had talked about her horseback excursions in other letters, and not only to Johanna. Clearly, Katrina was a skilled rider, since she—Abby stopped reading and stared, unseeing, at the bookshelves. Skilled rider. Katrina.

The night Ichabod disappeared, villagers reported sightings of the horseman. "Right there," Abby whispered. "It was right there the whole time." She went back through her notes for the past three boxes. She'd recorded each time Katrina mentioned a horseback ride. Which was fairly often and included long trips, sometimes with descriptions of the feats Katrina engaged in while riding.

It would have been easy for Katrina to dress as the horseman and ride around the glen. She'd been born and raised there and she rode around it all the time. She probably could do it with her vision obscured in a costume designed to make it look like a rider didn't have a head.

"A diversion," Abby said to her notes. She wanted to jump up and down at this possibility, but she restrained herself.

It made sense. In order to ensure that Ichabod disappeared without anyone noticing, Katrina made an appearance as the horseman. That alone would be enough to keep attention off one guy slipping out of the glen in the dark. She reached for her phone, wanting to text Katie this new idea, but she stopped before she picked it up. Friend zone. She stared at her phone. But they talked all the time about the legend. So why shouldn't she text her this latest theory? She pulled her hand back. Whatever. She'd see Katie later that evening.

Instead, Abby imagined Katrina getting her outfit ready, preparing to ride that night. The horse didn't necessarily have to be big and black. It could have been a dark color and that would have been enough to make people think that the Hessian rode again. In her dream from the previous night, Katrina had been on a big, black horse, at least for a moment. Weird, what the subconscious did. Katie had even said that the festival rider was sometimes a woman. She'd said something about how it worked out, because it was all about the illusion.

That's what Katrina did that night over two centuries ago. She created an illusion to help Ichabod disappear. And Elizabeth was in on it somehow. Finally. This might be a breakthrough in the parts of the legend that had remained hidden to her until this point. Abby wished again that Johanna had kept a really intimate journal and that it was available to researchers. Maybe Lu would find it filed away somewhere. Abby went through another folder. About halfway through, she stopped, struck by another thought. If Katrina was attracted to Ichabod—and her correspondence to Johanna suggested she was—how could she strike up a relationship with Elizabeth so soon after he left? Unless

Katrina was doing them both. Abby giggled at the thought of Katrina as an eighteenth-century player.

Lu appeared at the door. "Fifteen minutes before closing."

Abby looked up, surprised. "Thanks. Glad you reminded me."

"I have to have reminders, too, when I'm researching. See you in a bit." She retreated and Abby started putting the files carefully away. When she'd packed the box, she saved her notes and shut down her laptop. A few minutes later she placed the box on the front counter along with her open laptop bag for checking. Lu took the box back to storage and Abby saw that she already had her own bags ready to go.

"Katie tells me she's taking you to the glen tonight," Lu said upon her return.

Abby stifled a laugh because it sounded like something a parent might say to a teenager who had a date. "Yes. She, uh, said that she knows some spots where we'll be able to see the horseman." She remembered the car with the fogged-up windows from the other night and felt heat on her neck. That would be embarrassing, if Lu caught her blushing. Fortunately, Lu was busy putting some things away under the counter.

"She loves the festival," Lu said. "Has ever since the first time I took her when she was barely able to walk." She put her jacket on and placed her bags by the front door. Abby waited for her as Lu set the alarm.

"Is it true that women sometimes ride as the horseman?" She asked outside while Lu locked up.

"Probably." Lu picked up her bags and started walking. "Nobody knows who the rider is year to year, though we all have our guesses. It adds to the fun, not knowing, so nobody tries too hard to find out. Do you ride?"

"No. Never learned." Abby matched her pace to Lu's. Lots of people were out this afternoon. A group of kids across the street laughed and shouted and one chased the others, moaning.

"Katie rode, when she was younger. She enjoyed it, but never wanted to have a horse. Too much work and she enjoyed other sports more."

"So I guess the people who ride in the festival probably have horses. That would narrow down the identities, wouldn't it?"

Lu chuckled. "Maybe. Rumor is that some of the riders come from other communities nearby, which, if true, helps with the mystery. But around here, probably half the population has a horse."

"So you're saying it would probably be a dead end if I went around trying to find out about the secret horseman society for my dissertation."

Lu laughed. "Yes, it probably would."

A group of teenagers rode past in a station wagon, whooping and honking.

"It gets a little exciting around here on festival day," Lu said, still smiling.

"I can tell."

"Here's my turn. Have fun tonight. Hopefully, you'll see a few things and you can tell me all about them on Monday."

"Yeah. See you then." Abby continued walking, enjoying the anticipation percolating beneath the laughter and shouts of kids and teens, already in costume. Local businesses were giving out candy and she smiled, glad that she was here to celebrate, and especially glad that she'd be doing that with Katie. A secret crush was still kind of fun, she decided, even if she was relegated to the friend zone.

In the meantime, she had some time to organize the day's materials and think further about her latest theory.

"This is pretty good," Abby conceded after her first bite of the burger.

"Told you." Katie licked ketchup off her lip, and Abby tore her gaze away. Friend zone, she reminded herself.

They'd managed to score a place to sit on the low wall that surrounded the commemorative obelisk dedicated to the town's founders. The Van Tassel and Van Brunt names featured prominently. Weird but cool, how a descendant of both families over two hundred years later was sitting here in the town they founded.

"I have a new theory," Abby said between bites, surreptitiously admiring how good Katie looked in jeans. She had a gray SUNY-Binghamton T-shirt on under her dark blue fleece jacket.

"Spill it."

"Katrina masqueraded as the horseman the night Ichabod disappeared."

Katie stopped chewing. She took a sip of soda. "That's brilliant," she said after she swallowed. "That's even better than Katrina orchestrating a sighting."

"It kind of makes sense, right?"

"Totally. If they were trying to get Ichabod out of Sleepy Hollow for whatever reasons, create a diversion like that." She fell silent for a few moments. "And Katrina rode all the time. Shit, it was right there in her letters. All along."

"I thought the same thing." Abby took another bite and watched as a kid dressed like Ironman ran past, chased by another one dressed as The Hulk. The street and sidewalks were packed with people wandering among the vendors selling food and local craft products. It made her a little claustrophobic, but at least the vibe was focused on fun.

"I love that," Katie said. "I think that's my favorite theory so far."

"It's just a theory, but the circumstantial evidence lends itself to it."

Katie laughed. "Why, yes, Dr. Crane, it does."

Abby smiled. "Not a doctor yet."

"Fine. Master Crane—wait. Or would it be Mistress?"

"That sounds kinky."

Katie's eyebrows shot up. "Not that there's anything wrong with that."

Abby almost spit out her iced tea. She laughed and coughed at the same time, and Katie handed her a napkin.

"But we still don't know what the deal is with Elizabeth," Katie said.

"Besides the fact that she was hot n' heavy with Katrina?"

"Exactly. We don't know where she came from or where she went after Katrina died."

Abby finished her burger and put the wrapper in the bag it came in. "And it's weird, how Katrina was all into Ichabod and then she wasn't."

"Because he probably didn't die." Katie finished her burger, as well, and added her wrapper to the bag.

"So he's still alive and Katrina knows it, then Elizabeth shows up and Katrina was all, 'hottie' so she was doing them both?"

Katie laughed. "She got all sexy-time back in the day. And Mistress Van Tassel does have a nice ring to it." She finished her drink and put the empty cup in the bag. "Historic love triangle. Or threesome."

"I'm not sure how I feel about that."

"What? Sex back in the day?"

"No, not that. It's just that—would Katrina have risked that kind of situation, given the size of the community and the standing of her family? People paid attention to reputation and saving face. She might have been having affairs with two different people, but I think it would've been hard to pull off a love triangle of any kind in Sleepy Hollow." She put her empty cup in the bag, too.

"Good points. So maybe Ichabod left so that the three of them *could* pull off a polyamorous relationship. And I cannot believe I just used that term in a conversation about the legends of Sleepy Hollow."

Abby giggled. "Geek looks good on you."

"I'm glad. Because I actually am one."

"I like geeks." Especially ones that affected her like Katie.

"Lucky for me. And you're about to get even more geek, because it's time to go stake out a spot in the glen." She stood and held out her hand, and Abby took it automatically. Katie pulled her to her feet and grabbed the bag of trash with her free hand.

Abby's heartbeat sped up when she realized she was actually still holding Katie's hand, and it was warm in hers and made all kinds of sparks race up and down her arm.

Katie slowly pulled her hand away, and the expression in her eyes was unreadable.

Abby cleared her throat. "Um, there's a trash can right over there."

Katie disposed of the bag. "Ready?" she asked when she returned.

"Yeah. Let's go see some Sleepy Hollow lore in action." She walked next to Katie, both of them weaving through the crowds.

"How many people come to this?" Abby asked.

"Hundreds. Maybe more. And there's a bad-ass haunted house, so lots of people go to that. And they go run around the cemetery."

"Glad I have a local to show me around, then."

They arrived at Katie's SUV, parked in front of the bed and breakfast. Abby got in and buckled up.

"Did you bring a hat and gloves?" Katie asked as she started the engine. "It gets cold out there this time of year. I have extras if you didn't." She gestured at the back seat.

"Yep." Abby patted the zipper pockets of her fleece, but thought it would be nice, to wear something of Katie's. Oh, well.

She contented herself with stealing glances at Katie as she drove.

The sides of the road were lined with cars, and Katie had to go slow to avoid the groups of people walking toward the glen, some of whom were hard to see in the dark.

"How does the horseman even have room to ride around?" Abby asked as Katie slowed to a stop.

"Cars aren't allowed in the glen tonight, which helps keep the pathways and main road through it clear. Most people give him lots of room."

"Right. Wouldn't want to piss off a Hessian soldier, after all."

"Exactly." Katie pulled off the road, maneuvering between two other parked cars. "The township opens these fields for parking. There are donation buckets to help with any damages."

"Wow. People in Sleepy Hollow are so civilized during their festivals."

"Seemed the best solution as word spread." She stopped and turned off the engine. "And the city will actually close some of the roads into town tonight until about eleven, which means people who don't make it before six have to park outside city limits and walk or shuttle in. Helps keep things a little more organized." She got out and Abby did, too.

Katie continued, "It's about a quarter-mile into the glen, but we'll go around onto a different path." She slung a small backpack across one of her shoulders.

"Sounds good." Prickles of excitement shot down Abby's spine, but she wasn't sure if it was because she would be out here in the dark with Katie or because she was about to see the living embodiment of a legend that had played such a huge role in her family history.

Katie waited for her, and they walked on the main road for about ten minutes, passing several small groups of people, some with small children. A smaller road split to the left, and Katie took that, moving between still more groups of people. She stopped after another ten minutes at a barely discernible path to the right. It was nearly fully dark, and if Katie hadn't been with her, Abby would've kept walking.

"Here we go," Katie said. She took a small Maglite out of her backpack and turned it on. It joined bunches of others on the dirt road behind them, lights bouncing in the darkness like fireflies. "Stay close," she instructed as the path entered the glowering forests of the glen.

Abby did, since they couldn't walk side-by-side.

They passed a few people, but for the most part, they had the path to themselves as it twisted and turned deeper into the glen. Abby heard voices and laughter echoing through the darkness, and the beams from myriad flashlights glanced off trees, but most of the thrill-seekers were dozens of yards away. A child cried from somewhere ahead—or was it behind?—and somebody else yelled "Boo!", but it wasn't anywhere near them. The forest did strange things with sound.

They emerged into a clearing and Katie crossed it, picking up the path on the other side. "Careful," she said. "Big branch down." She went first then held the flashlight so Abby could step over it. "Almost there," she assured, and moments later, Abby glimpsed a line of flashlights ahead.

"They're standing along one of the main routes through the glen," Katie said. "We're going left a little bit because there's kind of a bypass over there that the horseman takes practically every year. People don't like to wait in here, especially if they have kids, because it's hard to see and move around. Hard to set up lawn chairs, too."

"Seriously? Lawn chairs?" Sacrilege. That seemed disrespectful, like watching it on TV. It defeated the purpose of being out here in the glen on a spooky night.

"I know, right? I prefer experiencing it without stuff like that. Okay, here's the bypass." She shone her flashlight on another hard-packed path, about twice as wide as the one they were on. "Do you mind hanging out right over there? We can sit on that tree."

Abby followed the beam of Katie's flashlight. A large tree had fallen just off the path, creating a nice bench. The main road was about a hundred feet away, separated from their position by trees and underbrush. "Sure." She headed over and sat down. The trunk was probably a good foot-and-a-half in diameter.

Katie took her backpack off and sat beside Abby.

"What time is it?" she asked as she unzipped her pack.

Abby checked her phone. "A little after eight."

"Perfect. He usually starts riding between eight-thirty and nine. Want some coffee?" She pulled a thermos and two plastic mugs out of her pack.

"Aren't you the Girl Scout? Yes."

Katie set the pack on the ground and unscrewed the top of the thermos. She poured some coffee into a mug, and handed it to Abby. "Hope you don't mind. It's already got cream and sugar."

"That'll work." Abby sipped. It was just shy of hot, but it was rich and strong. Great. She even had a crush on Katie's coffee.

Katie poured herself a cup and put the thermos away. "Okay if I turn the flashlight off?"

"Yes." There were plenty of others around the glen. She heard people moving through the forest, and picked up snatches of conversation from the people gathered on the road, about fifty feet away.

Katie turned the light off and Abby was even more aware of her proximity, as if the flashlight beam had been a boundary between them.

"It's pretty out here, even at night," Abby said, because the silence between them felt a little suggestive.

"I've always thought so. Maybe a little creepy, but I guess in a weird way I've always thought of the horseman as family. Kinda sick, maybe."

"No, that makes sense. He's been here as long as your family has." She sipped. "He's like that one not-quite-right uncle everybody has."

"Oh, yeah. The one without the head. All family trees have one."

Abby laughed. "That one or the one that disappeared."

"Definitely. One of those, too."

A kid screamed then laughed in delight from the main road. Night enveloped the forest, though flashlight beams pierced it as people moved around and prepared for the spectacle.

"So how easy would it be for me to talk to someone who's ridden as the horseman?" Abby asked.

"Not very. But go ahead and try."

"And you don't know any of the horsemen?"

"Nope. Or the horsewomen, either. I've had an idea or two about them over the years, but that's one secret I think I'd like to stay hidden. It adds another layer of mystique to the glen."

"Do you think that people have been dressing up as the horseman this whole time?"

"What do you mean?"

"Well, if Katrina did in fact ride as the horseman that night when Ichabod disappeared, it stands to reason that other people have done it over the years, too. As a way to keep the legend alive, you know?" Abby wrapped her hands around the cup, enjoying the lingering warmth from the coffee within.

"It's possible. But what about Gary's story? That doesn't sound like a fake horseman."

Abby considered his description of the horseman, which was a lot like in her dream.

"And why would you want to do it?" Katie shifted on the tree trunk, and her thigh pressed against Abby's.

"Who knows? People are strange." Abby gripped her cup harder. Katie hadn't moved her leg away and Abby was only too aware of the warmth she felt against her own. "I mean, maybe this whole dressing up as the horseman has a much longer history than the 1980s."

"Okay, I'll buy that. So if Katrina pretended to be the horseman that night, then maybe other people did, too. Including women."

"Absolutely. Why wouldn't they? And what a cool idea, to feel invincible for a minute, riding around knowing that nobody is going to mess with you." Abby took another sip of coffee, gripping the cup hard in both hands. Katie still hadn't moved her leg away and Abby was pretty sure people might mistake her heartbeat for the horseman.

"I love that idea," Katie said. "A kind of feminist rebellion by dressing up as a headless male ghost—are you cold?"

"Uh, not really." Abby was trembling a little, but not from the chill. She made a show of moving like she needed to shift her position and she put a little space between her leg and Katie's. Not that she wanted to. But right now, it was probably for the best.

"Let me know if you are. I have one of those space blanket things."

"Total Girl Scout."

"I actually preferred the Boy Scouts. They got to do a lot of cool stuff. I used to think it would be fun to dress like a boy and participate."

"Exactly my point. Women have been dressing like guys for centuries. Katrina may have done it to play the horseman, but so many other women did it to live independent lives. Like those women who dressed as men and served in the Civil

War—" She stopped. "Oh, my God. What if the Hessian was actually a woman?" She turned to Katie automatically and her thigh again touched Katie's. She kept it there, hoping that the conversation would keep her from thinking too much about the effect Katie had on her.

"Stop. Just stop," Katie said, half-laughing. "Because that would be amazing."

"It's possible. Women served as men in the Revolutionary War, too. Like Deborah Sampson. Who actually served in battle in this area."

"Okay, mind blown."

"Women masqueraded as men all the time historically," Abby continued. "Sometimes just so they could live sort of openly with other women. Not as themselves, obviously, but—"

"Oh, my God."

"What?" Abby stopped and listened. Was it time for the horseman? But all she heard were laughter and voices and the sounds of lots of spectators.

"What you just said. Why the hell didn't we think about that before?"

"What do you mean?"

"Don't you see?" Katie put her hand on Abby's forearm. "Women dressing as men historically. We know of a few instances, but think of all the instances we *don't* know. Lots, probably."

"And?" Abby asked, puzzled.

"Ichabod."

"Ichabod what?"

"Maybe Ichabod wasn't a man."

"Oh, my God." A woman. Abby had to remind herself to breathe. Ichabod might have been a woman.

"What if that was the secret Katrina mentioned?"

Abby stared into the dark, barely aware that Katie's hand was still on her arm. "Both elated and distressed." She quoted from Katrina's letter to Johanna.

"So if Ichabod was a woman, Katrina was not disgusted by that," Katie said. "She was elated—could be she preferred women. Hell, she liked Elizabeth, after all."

"And maybe she was distressed because she knew what would happen to Ichabod if anybody else found out." Abby turned toward her, and could just make out her features in the dark. Her vision had adjusted.

"That makes a good reason to help someone disappear."

"I think my mind is blown, too." Abby sipped her coffee, using one hand to lift it, so she wouldn't have to move her arm out of Katie's grasp, which felt really good. The coffee was nearly cold. She finished it.

Katie's grip tightened. "Listen," she said, her voice just above a whisper.

"I don't hear anything."

"That's the point. Everybody's quieted down. It's starting." She released Abby's arm and stood. Abby handed over her mug and Katie quickly packed.

As Katie shrugged into the pack's straps, Abby got up and glanced toward the main road, where flashlight beams continued to slice through the darkness. The crowd had hushed, the eerie quiet only broken by sporadic nervous laughter and a restless child speaking too loudly.

"Listen," Katie said again.

Abby did, and she thought she heard a faint pounding, like someone beating in a regular pattern on a drum. From farther away, she heard cheers and screams.

"He's coming," Katie said, and Abby felt Katie's fingers intertwine with hers.

Abby didn't pull away. In fact, she moved a little closer.

"I think he's on the opposite side from where we came in," Katie said, and her lips were very close to Abby's ear.

Chills shot down Abby's spine, and not because of the approaching horseman.

The sound of pounding increased and Abby thought about the first dream she'd had since she'd been here. She concentrated on her feet and the ground beneath, but the thick forest loam must've muted the approaching horse because she didn't feel the vibrations like she did in her dream.

People started cheering from the nearby main road, and Abby stared as a dark shape hurtled past the crowds that lined either side. She caught only glimpses of it between the trees, but Katie was pulling her.

"Come on. There's a little more open space over here."

Abby let Katie guide her a few feet along the path until they were almost to the main road. Seconds later, probably because they were standing on the hard-packed path, she felt vibrations in her feet.

A horse's hooves, pounding.

The crowd cheered again, a low roar that drowned out the sound of the horseman's approach, but not the feel. And then there he was, at the point where the bypass met the main road, the big black horse pawing at the earth, puffs of its breath showing in the beams of flashlights that skidded across its hide and the form of the horseman, which did not have a visible head. And then the horse shot forward onto the bypass to the cheers and shouts of the crowd.

Abby heard the creak of leather, the click of the bit in the horse's mouth and the horse's deep breathing as they passed, but no sound from the headless rider. As it should be, she thought, and she caught the smell of horse. Nothing dank or musty. Just the odor of animal and maybe hay. Like a barn.

"Wow," she said as the horseman disappeared down the bypass. She could tell when he left it, because of the cheers from the crowd.

"He is pretty cool," Katie said. "He'll do another few passes on the main road. Do you want to watch?"

"Yeah," she said, distracted by the warmth of Katie's hand and the feel of their connection as Katie pulled her along the path.

Katie managed to position them along the main road in front of a group of taller guys who were giving each other high-fives. They had an unobstructed view of the road, and for that she was glad because the horseman made another pass, right down the middle of the road. The roar from the crowd drowned out the sound of the horse's hooves but the horseman stopped a few feet away from Abby and made the horse turn in a few jittery circles.

Several people had their flashlight beams trained on him, and flashes from cameras and phones added a strange effect, like a light show at a concert. The rider urged his horse into a near-gallop, much to the delight of the crowd, and took off, going in the direction of the parking area Katie had used the first time she'd brought Abby to the glen.

"What do you think?" Katie asked. "Was it worth the trip?"

"Definitely." It dawned on her that she was still holding hands with Katie, but it felt so nice that she didn't pull away.

Shouts and screams erupted from the other side of the road and a few dozen feet away.

"He's in the forest," someone yelled.

"Oh, cool," Katie said. "It's one of the better riders."

And then the horseman exploded out of the woods on the other side of the road, scattering the crowd.

Katie said something, but Abby couldn't hear her over the shouting from the crowd as the horseman beelined for the bypass, the horse panting loud enough to hear. The guys behind them surged forward and Katie's hand slipped out of Abby's as they were separated. Abby stood now in the middle of the road as the horseman approached. She backed up, thinking he was going to need room to get around her but instead he turned down the bypass again. Several people in the crowd followed, cheering, but Abby remained in the road. Crowds made her nervous.

"Abby." Katie's voice, right behind her. "Are you okay?"

"Yeah. That was crazy." Abby turned toward her.

"And a little dangerous. Not nearly as good as some of the others who ride through the forest. Whoever that is better hope I don't catch him."

Spectators were resuming positions along the side of the road after the earlier excitement. Somebody bumped into her. "Sorry," he said.

Abby pressed closer to Katie.

"Are you ready to leave?" Katie asked, concern in her voice.

"No. I'm just not a fan of crowds."

"This way." Katie guided her until they came to a path that jagged to the left, the same one they'd walked to a couple nights ago. Abby followed Katie onto the path, keeping her eye on the flashlight beam. A few people passed and exchanged greetings, but it was much less crowded here than on the main road through the glen.

Katie slowed and kept her flashlight trained on the ground. "This'll meet up with another path that'll take us to the one we came in on. Most people stick to the main road during the ride because it's easier. The horseman will be riding the periphery now, which is why everybody's headed out."

"I can see how people manufacture stories, even if the horseman hasn't been a real ghost all these years." Abby took her knit hat out of one of her pockets and put it on. She put her hands into the pockets of her fleece.

"It is pretty convincing."

"And imagine it's a night like tonight. No electricity, so everything's black. The only light you have might be a torch or a lantern. And here comes this dark thing out of the woods—that's enough for a legend."

Cheers floated on the breeze. Abby shivered.

"He's riding the periphery now," Katie said.

"Sounds like it."

Voices sounded behind them and they stood aside for a group of young people clearly trying to get out of the glen. Their flashlight beams bobbed in the dark. Abby glanced behind them but saw nobody else.

"This place clears out fast, for the number of people that were here," Abby said.

"They'll try to catch more sightings on the periphery and then go back to town for more festival stuff. Lots of businesses downtown stay open until midnight."

More cheers, this time from a different direction, and farther away.

"It's easier for him to ride fast out there than it is in the glen. Not so many trees."

"Which means Katrina was an outstanding horsewoman, to ride through here back then," Abby said.

"Speaking of which, I'm really liking the idea that Ichabod was a woman."

"It's a great idea. And it makes sense, since Katrina's descriptions of him talk about how he's 'delicate of feature'. Plus, he was all about teaching women to read. Maybe he went undercover so he could talk like that without facing the kind of sanctions that women had to deal with then."

"So we might have Ichabod and Katrina figured out. We still don't have Elizabeth figured out though," Katie said. "What's her role in this, besides being Katrina's other lover?"

"I don't know. Still thinking about that." And where did Elizabeth come from? It was like Katrina flipped a switch in her correspondence, and Elizabeth just appeared.

"How long are you in town?" Katie asked, breaking Abby's train of thought.

"I'm heading back Tuesday morning. You?"

"Same." Katie didn't say anything else for a few moments. "Do you think you'll have all the material you need?"

"No. I'm planning on coming back."

"Let me know when you do. I'll see if I can get here, too, and we can theorize some more."

"We can do that anyway. There're these things called phones. And this other thing called the Internet," Abby teased, trying not to sound overeager.

"Yeah, but it's more fun in person." She stopped and Abby did, too. "I've been having a great time hanging out with you," Katie said, and though the flashlight was pointed at the ground, there was enough of a glow from it that Abby could see Katie's face.

"Me, too. Hanging out with you, I mean. Not hanging out with myself. I do that all the time," she finished, wincing inwardly because it sounded dorky.

Katie smiled and the air seemed to spark between them. So maybe this wasn't a friend zone? Katie took Abby's hand again and pulled her a little closer. Oh, no. Definitely not a friend zone. Abby's heartbeat sped up and delightful chills raced up her back as Katie leaned in.

And then the pounding of hoofbeats sounded, not more than a few dozen feet away.

Abby turned to look back down the path. A huge dark horse was fast approaching. She instinctively grabbed Katie's arm and pulled her out of the way. The horse barreled past— the only sound, its hooves. Abby caught a glimpse of the headless rider and what might've been a sword at the rider's side and maybe the glint of—brass? Buttons?—and then the shape seemed to meld with the darkness that pooled beneath the trees on either side of the path.

"What the hell are you doing?" Katie yelled after the rider. "It's damn dangerous to pull crap like that."

Abby stared in the direction the rider had gone. She listened, but no longer heard hoofbeats. Instead, she heard the distant cheering of the crowd. "Something's not right," she said.

"Definitely not. This year's rider is an asshole." Katie started walking again, and Abby silently cursed the horseman for interrupting a really hot moment. But something was wrong.

She felt the pounding through her shoes before she heard it, like in her dream. "Katie," she said. "Get off the path." She grabbed her hand and pulled her again into the forest.

"Shit," Katie yelled as the horseman galloped past, headed in the opposite direction he had gone the first time. "What the hell is he doing? And why isn't he on the periphery?"

Abby heard more cheers in the distance. "I think the horseman *is* on the periphery. This is another one."

Katie was quiet for a few moments until the distant cheering subsided and then picked up again. "Two horsemen? What the hell is that about?"

"Has it happened before? Maybe two ride every once in a while to cover more ground."

"I don't know. I guess I never thought about it," Katie said as she took Abby back onto the path and they resumed walking, though their pace was faster now. "Either way, I still say this one is an asshole."

Katie took Abby's hand again, which was more comforting at that moment than arousing. Abby kept glancing over her shoulder, though it made her stumble a couple of times. She was shivering, but it wasn't because she was cold.

Again, Abby felt hoofbeats before she heard them, and every hair on the back of her neck stood straight out. "Katie," she said, urgent. She stopped and stared behind her. A shape in the darkness down the path seemed to morph into a horse and rider, approaching fast. Really fast.

"Katie," Abby yelled. "Get down." She threw herself against Katie and they both hit the ground, Abby on top. She felt something move above her and she opened her eyes, as a dark shape sailed over them to land without a sound. As it moved away, though, she heard hoofbeats.

"You dick," Katie yelled after him, still underneath Abby, who scrambled to her feet.

"Are you okay?" Abby asked.

"Just pissed. You?"

"Pissed and scared." Abby helped her up and they both stood still, listening. More cheering from somewhere near where they had parked, Abby guessed from the sounds. But she couldn't be sure.

"Anything?" Abby asked after a while.

"No. That asshole had better be gone."

They walked in silence, Abby grateful for the wan light from the finally risen moon that found its way to the path. She refused to glance over her shoulder, even though she was sure something was behind them. She tripped on what was probably a tree root, but Katie caught her.

"Okay?" Katie asked.

"Yeah. Just freaked out."

"Me, too. But I'm still really pissed and that douche better hope that I don't ever find out who the hell he is."

"I'm right there with you." Abby heard cheers in the distance and that somehow made her feel a little better. She looked around, the moonlight both helping and hindering, because it caused weird shadows that seemed to move.

"Anything?" Katie asked.

"Nothing behind us."

"Good. Nothing in front, either. And we're almost to the path we took to get in here."

"That makes me really happy."

"Same here."

And though the path had narrowed and Abby had to walk just behind, Katie took her hand and stayed close. Abby heard laughter in the woods on both sides and saw flashlight beams. They also caught up to a group of three people on the same path, two women and a man.

"Hey," the man said. "Fun night in the glen."

"Yeah," Katie's response sounded forced.

"Great rider this year," one of the women added.

Abby squeezed Katie's hand and fought an urge to laugh. If she started, she probably wouldn't stop. "Definitely," she said as Katie pulled her past them.

When they arrived at the SUV, Abby climbed in and sank gratefully into the seat. She took her hat off and stuffed it into one of her jacket pockets.

Katie closed her door and started the engine. "I'm freezing," she said as she turned the heat on.

Cool air blew onto Abby and she closed the vents in the dashboard closest to her.

"It'll warm up in a minute." Katie didn't pull back onto the road and that was fine with Abby, since there were cars merging onto it from both sides, moving very slowly around groups of people.

"Okay, so, what the hell happened out there?" Katie asked after a while.

Abby opened the vents because she felt heat on her legs. "Two riders. And according to my scientific calculations, one is clearly a dick."

Katie laughed, and it sounded relieved. "Clearly."

"I'm taking a cautious and scientific approach about this topic."

"And I respect that."

"The one who was a dick had a sword. The other didn't." Abby leaned forward and put one hand over the vent in the dashboard near the window. "Another alternative is that we might just have seen the ghost of a Hessian soldier over two hundred years old. However, I'm not sure how I feel about that."

"Me, either. So chances are it was a very human asshole."

Abby placed her other hand over the vent. "I'd consider the possibility that I might not have seen what I thought I saw. My brain might have manufactured something extra scary, given the circumstances."

"True. The brain manufactures all kinds of things." Katie slowed to a near-crawl behind another vehicle that was trying to get around a group of pedestrians. "And we have been kind of obsessing over this story for the past few days."

"Speak for yourself. I've been *completely* obsessing."

Katie laughed.

"I even had a couple of weird dreams."

"Oh? Do tell."

Abby did, and when she finished, she felt less freaked out by what had happened.

"So both Katrina and the rider showed up in your dreams." Katie was finally able to speed up, though they hadn't made it to the paved road yet.

"And Katrina showed up once as the rider. But she was herself, and not in disguise."

"Interesting, that you dreamed about Katrina riding a horse," Katie said. "Especially if she did play the horseman that night Ichabod disappeared."

"It's kind of weird. Maybe it was an idea in my subconscious that I hadn't accessed yet." Abby put her hands in her jacket pockets, more to keep them to herself than that they were cold. The vehicle had warmed up, but she'd almost taken Katie's hand while she was telling her about the dreams, and she wasn't sure how that would go over, now that they were in this different context.

A driver flashed his lights, indicating that she could pull in front of him. Katie opened her window and waved at him then closed it. "Brr," she said. Her phone rang and she pulled it out of the inside pocket of her jacket. "It's Lu."

Abby nodded and stared out the window as Katie talked. She thought about how she almost kissed Katie—just like an asshole headless horseman, to interrupt that. She bit back a laugh.

"Lu wants to know if we want to come by for a bit," Katie said to her. "She's having some people over. Hot drinks. Snacks," she added, coaxing.

"I'm in." It would probably help put the evening into perspective, though being pissed at whoever it was for ruining a nice moment helped wash the creepy out, too.

"Cool." Katie resumed talking to Lu and Abby settled back, the warmth from the heater vents making her a little sleepy. By the time they got to Lu's—a historic bungalow with a wide, covered porch—she was even more relaxed, and the evening's events sat a little easier in the back of her mind. Maybe they'd fade even more after a party. Might as well try. She followed Katie inside.

Ghosts

"Two riders?" Lu looked at Katie then Abby. "Are you sure?"

"Well, the evidence is anecdotal." Katie flashed a smile at Abby. "But we heard cheering from the periphery of the glen while we were dealing with the dick *in* the glen."

"And the first rider didn't have a sword. The second that was in the glen with us did," Abby added. She sipped her wine.

The three of them had ended up in camp chairs in the back yard next to Lu's outdoor fire pit. The remaining logs glowed and one popped and sent a shower of sparks into the air. The heat radiated off Abby's legs, and this setting made the events in the glen seem far away. She was so relaxed that she might fall asleep out here.

"That's very strange." Lu stretched her hands to the fire. "But I suppose it's probably happened over the years."

"Whoever it was, he'd better hope I don't find out who he is. You should have seen him, racing up and down on a horse. The damn path was barely wide enough for two people to stand next to each other." Katie took a swallow from her beer bottle.

"There's always a chance of something going wrong, but that sounds more reckless than it needed to be," Lu said.

"Exactly. What if we'd had a kid with us or something? Or somebody had a ninety-year-old out there?"

Lu laughed. "Well, I don't think a ninety-year-old is going to be traipsing around the glen like that at night. But thank you for your concern for children and senior citizens."

Abby smiled. "So if you have some kind of grapevine to the secret horseman society, Lu, tell them we're trying to save children and senior citizens from practical jokers who act like assholes in the glen during the annual festival."

"I'll see what I can do," she said, and it sounded like she wasn't kidding. She stood. "Do either of you want something else to drink?"

Katie held her bottle up in the light from the fire pit, inspecting it. "No. I'm good."

"I'm fine," Abby said. "I still have half a glass."

"All right. Put another log on if you want, Katie." Lu went back inside.

Light spilled through the windows onto the back porch, which looked like someone had added it on in the last few years. Like the front porch, it was covered, and it held a wrought iron table and chairs.

"This is a great house," Abby said as she turned her gaze back to Katie. And she'd been right about a historic bungalow as the type of house Lu would live in.

"Yeah. Always feels good here. Speaking of, how are you doing?"

"Better. And you?"

"Same. I feel kind of bad that it happened, though. I hope it didn't scar you for life."

Abby laughed. "Not even close."

"So does that mean that you'll maybe want to go again at some point?"

"I'll need a local guide." Abby stretched her legs out.

"I know someone who is really interested in that position."

"Then I think we can work something out." She looked over at Katie, and she thought about the moment they'd shared in the glen, and she wished she had managed to kiss her. Then again, maybe she was glad they hadn't. Maybe the asshole had done them a favor, because she wouldn't have been able to savor the aftermath of a kiss with Katie with the horseman galloping up and down that path. She really hoped they'd have another chance.

"So—" Katie started.

"Did either of you want some hot chocolate?" Lu called from the back door.

"No, thanks," both Katie and Abby said at the same time. Abby heard more voices and she looked at the back door just as a couple of guys and a woman came outside. So much for privacy.

"It's almost midnight," Katie said. She put her phone back in her jacket pocket. "I'm going to guess that you're tired. I know I am." The newcomers sat down in the empty camp chairs on the other side of the fire pit and Katie greeted them. Abby just smiled and offered a little wave.

"Yeah," Abby said to Katie. "I am."

"Ready to go?"

Abby nodded and forced herself to stand. Definitely tired. But disappointed, too. She'd wanted a little more time with Katie.

"Later," Katie said to the others as she and Abby went inside. Lu was in the kitchen, working on hot chocolate.

"Hey, Lu. We're both really tired." Katie put her beer bottle and Abby's glass on the counter. "I'm going to take Abby back to Eleanor's and I'll probably see you Monday."

"All right, sweetie." Lu gave her a hug and a kiss. "When are you leaving on Tuesday?"

"In the morning."

"Okay." Lu looked at Abby. "I'll see you on Monday. Come early."

"I will. Thanks." She waved at Lu before she joined Katie at the front door. Nobody was on the front porch, and as Katie closed the door behind them, Abby reveled in the fact that she was finally alone with her, as tired as she was. Not much light fell through the windows here, since the front rooms of the house were mostly dark, but some emanated from four jack o' lanterns—two on the floor on each side of the doorway and two others on waist-high plant stands above them. Somebody must have put fresh candles in them, because lively flames still flickered through their eyes and mouths, and Abby caught the faint smell of charred pumpkin.

Katie made no move to leave the porch, so Abby stayed, watching her face in the glow from the jack o' lanterns.

Katie cleared her throat. "So, um, even though things got a little out of hand out there, I had a really good time."

"So did I. Thanks for taking me to the glen."

"Oh, sure. Glad I was able to facilitate something so scary that we both almost lost our shit."

Abby laughed. "Isn't that what Halloween's about? So this one is pretty memorable." And not just because of the glen.

"Definitely." Katie didn't say anything for a few seconds, and silence gathered between them, the kind filled with anticipation.

Katie eventually slid her hands into her jacket pockets. "What are you doing tomorrow?" she asked, and she sounded so endearing. There was something really delicious about that.

"I don't know. I haven't made any plans." Abby tried not to sound too hopeful.

"Um, so...would you like to get together?" Something in the tone of her voice released butterflies in Abby's chest. Definitely not a friend zone tone.

"If it involves the glen, I'm taking a rain check."

"Well, darn," Katie teased. "Okay, how about lunch?"

"That would be great."

"Good. That's really good. Um, because I'd really like to spend more time with you."

Abby's heart pounded and sparks danced down her legs. "So can I presume that you're officially asking me out?"

Katie half-laughed and it sounded nervous. "Yeah."

"And can I also presume that unlike your ancestor, you don't have any other people in the wings?"

Katie laughed. "Yes, you can presume that. I'm single and I'm not really the polyamorous type. If that was really what was going on with Katrina and company. We'll have to theorize more on that."

"I'd actually like to theorize on something else right now."

"Oh?"

Abby cupped Katie's cheeks with her hands, surprised at her own boldness, and leaned in. She barely touched her lips to Katie's, but she let them linger, because she liked how it felt, to go slow and light at first. But Katie's breath was hot and fast against her mouth and Abby felt Katie's hands on her hips. So Abby kissed her a little harder, and Katie responded, and oh, God, her lips were amazing. Better than she'd fantasized. So much better. Abby wrapped her arms around Katie and pulled her close, and the feel of Katie against her like that and Katie's mouth made Abby's blood heat, made her want much more.

Abby pulled away before she indulged that desire, but kept her arms around Katie's neck.

"Damn," Katie said softly, hands still on Abby's hips. "I'm going to hope that's a yes to going out on an official date with me."

"Definitely." Abby stared into Katie's eyes, reveling in what she saw within. She covered Katie's hands with her own. "And as much as I'd like to continue this, it's late, I'm tired, and we're standing on your aunt's porch."

Katie grinned. "True."

Abby took her hands off Katie's. And Katie let go of Abby's hips, though by the look in Katie's eyes, it was clear she didn't want to. She held Abby's hand on the way to the bed and breakfast, a too-short, eight-block drive. And now here they were, standing on the walk that led to the front door.

"Noon tomorrow?" Katie asked.

"Perfect."

"I'll pick you up." She took Abby's hand again, and they walked together up the walkway and up the steps that led to the bed and breakfast's wraparound porch. Katie waited while Abby got the key out of her pocket and unlocked the door.

"Good night," Katie said. "In spite of all the crazy, I had a most excellent evening."

Abby smiled. "Same here. See you soon." She fought an urge to kiss her again, because she knew if she did, she'd bring Katie inside. And as much as she wanted to do that, she preferred waiting a little. And she definitely wanted to be rested. Those thoughts made her thighs tingle. "Good night," she said, and she stepped inside and closed the door behind her before she could change her mind.

Katie waved at her through the door's glass and blew her a goofy kiss. Abby laughed and watched her until she had pulled away from the curb. A most excellent evening indeed. She went upstairs to bed.

Hardly any light filtered to the forest floor from the waning moon and Abby struggled to make out the path underfoot, which was barely wider than her two feet. She picked her way, mindful of where she stepped.

"Elizabeth," she heard a woman calling, her voice echoing through the otherwise silent forest.

Finally, she reached a clearing bathed in weak moonlight and there stood a figure in a black cloak.

"Elizabeth," the figure said as she pushed her cloak's hood back.

Katrina, Abby thought. Or did she say it aloud? She didn't hear herself speak, but Katrina approached.

"They mustn't see you like this, my love," Katrina said. "The trousers will no longer do."

My love? Abby looked down at her legs. She was wearing jeans. Katrina embraced her and Abby stiffened. I'm not Elizabeth, she tried to say, but the words never left her mouth. Why couldn't she talk? And were they in the glen? Would the horseman come?

"We must get you out of these clothes," Katrina said and suddenly she wasn't Katrina, but rather Katie, who wrapped them both in the cloak and Abby felt Katie's lips on her neck and then on her mouth and she was so safe and so warm and then Katie's phone rang.

Phone?

Abby opened her eyes then shut them again because the morning light was bright enough to hurt. The phone rang again, but it wasn't Katie's. It was the land line downstairs, and it was a loud, old-fashioned ring. She heard somebody answer, and she stretched and smiled as memories of last night's kiss replaced the dream and greeted her along with the sunlight. The bedside clock read a little after nine, and Abby groaned and covered her head with her pillow, thinking about the night before, remembering how Katie's lips made her feel like fireworks on a roller coaster.

The clock read nearly ten when she looked at it again so she got out of bed. She was halfway to the bathroom when her phone rang with a specific tone. "Hey," she answered, thinking that she finally understood what the term "swoon" meant.

"Hi," Katie said. "Sorry to bother you, but I just—I really wanted to hear your voice."

Abby smiled so wide it almost hurt. She sank back onto the bed. "And I'm so glad you did."

"And as I suspected would be the case, it's having an amazing effect on me."

"Is that a scientific assessment?"

"Absolutely not. Some things are beyond the reach of science."

Oh, God. Abby forced herself to breathe normally. How was this even happening? Things like this *never* happened to her. But here she was, in the middle of a crush gone live. "I agree. Some things are."

"So. Um. I was wondering if maybe we could start lunch a little earlier." Tentative. A little shy. Too cute.

"I can be ready in thirty minutes," Abby said.

"Late breakfast okay? Unless you're dying for more lunch-appropriate food."

"Breakfast is good any time of the day."

"I knew I liked you. Pancakes?"

"Love them."

"Then I have just the place. Totally casual. I'll see you in a bit."

Abby rolled off the bed. "Yes, you will. Bye."

"Bye."

Abby tossed the phone on the chair and did a little hop and jump while she pumped her fists in the air. Date. Thirty minutes. She bounded into the bathroom, took a quick shower, then agonized for another ten minutes about which pair of jeans to wear. She opted for the older, with the faded knees and butt, and put them on along with an old gray T-shirt over which she put her favorite rugby shirt, thinking about how good Katie looked dressed as casually as this.

Did she really kiss her last night? Her lips tingled with the memory. Yes. She had. And it was even better than her imagination had promised.

She laced her hiking shoes, thinking. Sometimes dreams tried to tell you something, but only because they were tapping into things already in your head that you hadn't yet accessed. So why would Katrina call her Elizabeth? And why would she tell her that the trousers would no longer do? She stood just as her cell phone dinged with a text message. Katie, letting her know she was outside. Abby grabbed her fleece, wallet, and room key and practically ran down the stairs and out the front door.

Katie's SUV was parked right in front on the street and she was leaning against the passenger side. When she saw Abby, she smiled and took her sunglasses off.

How could anyone look so good in jeans and a sweatshirt, Abby wondered. She'd left her hair down and it hung around her shoulders in soft, dark waves. Now *that* was a sight.

"Hi," she said as Abby approached, and she looked like she wasn't sure how to greet her, like she was debating how much physical contact she should display.

"Morning," Abby replied and solved Katie's dilemma by leaning in and kissing her on the cheek. Her lips lingered just a little longer than a friendly peck.

Katie touched the spot where Abby's lips had just been. The expression in her eyes was a mixture of pleasure, surprise, and relief.

"Pancake time," Abby said as she opened the passenger door.

"So it is." Katie went around to the driver's side. "How was your night?" she asked as she pulled away from the curb.

"Before or after you drove me to the bed and breakfast?" She looked over at Katie and was rewarded with another smile.

"If your night was anything like mine before that, then it was incredible." She kept her eyes on the road.

"So was mine." Abby stared out the windshield, too, enjoying the charge in the air between them but feeling a little shy herself all of a sudden. Katie didn't say anything for a while until they'd hit the outskirts of town, on a different road than the one to the glen.

"The restaurant is a few miles away, but it's really worth it," Katie said. "It might be a little crowded, since it's Sunday, but maybe everybody slept in." She drummed her fingers on the steering wheel, and fidgeted as she drove.

"Sounds good." Abby got a little more comfortable, giving Katie space to say whatever was on her mind, because she clearly needed it.

"Okay, here's the deal," Katie said a few moments later. "I've wanted to kiss you since Thursday, when I met you officially at the historical society."

The butterflies in Abby's stomach increased by at least a few hundred. "I would've let you." Which was crazy, but true.

"Yeah?" Katie looked at her.

"Road," Abby said as the SUV drifted into the other lane.

Katie steered back. "Sorry. You have this...*effect* on me." She smiled. "You would have?"

"Yes. I have no scientific explanation for it. And I'm not looking for one."

Another silence fell between them, but it was a shared assessment, and Abby welcomed it.

"So, um, I'd like to get to know you better," Katie said.

"I'd like that." Abby studied her profile and thoroughly enjoyed the view.

"But I might be a little old fashioned in some respects." Katie slowed down and turned left into the parking lot of a sprawling log structure that looked like it belonged on the label of a bottle of maple syrup. It had a fireplace or a stove because smoke curled from its chimney. Downright homey. And lucky for them, the lot was only half-full.

"Well, Gary did say you were picky," Abby said.

Katie laughed. "Oh, he did?" She parked and turned off the engine. "And maybe I hoped he'd find out whether or not you were single."

"He did find out. But you could've asked me," Abby said with a little grin.

"I might not have wanted to know if you weren't."

"Clearly." Abby opened her door.

"What do you mean?" Katie asked as she got out too, her tone light and teasing.

"From my observations Thursday in the glen, I'm pretty sure you would have been fine with it had something happened between us, regardless of my relationship status." Abby shot her another grin and walked to the restaurant's entrance.

"Guilty." Katie grinned back. "But I had a feeling you weren't involved." She moved ahead of Abby and held the door open for her.

"That's not very scientific of you."

"Some things, Mistress Crane, are way beyond the reach of science."

Abby laughed and went inside.

Two cups of coffee later, two huge plates of pancakes arrived. She was pretty sure this was the best date ever, sitting across from Katie in a booth in a funky log cabin diner-esque place that probably wasn't on any maps.

"I had another dream last night," Abby said after she took a bite. "And these pancakes must have some kind of addictive substance, because I'm not sure I'll be able to stop eating them."

"The secret's in the batter. But I'm not sure what exactly they do to it."

"Probably better not to know."

"Probably. So what was in the dream?" Katie sipped her coffee.

Abby told her between bites of pancake, but she left off the part where Katie showed up and kissed her into next week.

"Katrina wanted you to get out of your clothes?" Katie raised her eyebrows and smirked behind her coffee cup.

"Well, when you put it like that—"

"Do you remember exactly what dreamy Katrina said?"

"Um, 'We must get you out of these clothes.'"

"I see." Katie stifled a laugh.

"Wait. Before that, she said something to the effect of they mustn't see you in trousers." Abby frowned, trying to remember. "She called me Elizabeth and said the trousers will no longer do."

"So dreamy Katrina called you Ichabod in one of your dreams and in this most recent one she called you Elizabeth and said your trousers had to go." Katie grinned. "Katrina was definitely hot n' heavy."

Abby laughed. "I probably dreamed it because we'd been talking about women dressing as men, and you suggested that Ichabod might be a woman—" she stopped, staring at Katie. "Oh, my God."

"What?" Katie put her coffee cup down.

"Katrina called me Elizabeth in the one dream, Ichabod in the other."

"So?"

"And she wanted me to take my clothes off, but she was worried that someone would see me in my trousers. She wanted me to *change* my clothes. Not just take them off."

"Change to what?"

"A dress, I'd guess." It was right there. In the dream. And maybe sitting in one of the files in her brain, and she'd finally managed to access it.

"Why—" Katie stopped, then, and stared back at Abby. "No way."

"Think about what Irving wrote, and what they found after Ichabod disappeared. A bundle of his clothes and a couple of other things. Ichabod *was* a woman."

"*And* she was Elizabeth. What. The. Hell." Katie shook her head slowly.

"That's it. That's the one explanation that fits the historical record as Katrina recorded it. Ichabod disappears and Elizabeth shows up after that. Katrina never mentions Ichabod again, but she's all about Elizabeth. And Johanna knew. She knew everything." Abby picked up her coffee cup, but she was in a trance of sorts. "Ichabod was Elizabeth."

"It totally fits."

"Circumstantially, at least. And I have no scientific explanation as to why I got these answers in dreams."

"What else was in that dream last night? Maybe we can find out for sure about the asshole horseman." Katie handed her plate to the server.

Abby handed her plate over, too, but didn't answer until the server left. "The horseman wasn't in my dream last night." She thought about the dream's end and felt heat on her neck and hoped Katie didn't notice.

Katie laughed. "Hmm. From that blush, I'm guessing Katrina *did* get a little hot n' heavy in dreamland."

Damn. She'd seen it. Abby tried to be nonchalant. "You could say that." Someone named Katrina had done that in her dream, after all.

"Lucky for her." Katie poured more coffee from the pitcher they'd been sharing.

"The dream started with the historic Katrina, but ended with a different one. That was the one who might've gotten a little, um..." she cleared her throat.

Katie stopped stirring her coffee and caught Abby's gaze, a little smile at the corners of her mouth. "Really. Anyone I know?"

She was teasing, Abby knew, but she gave Katie a pointed look anyway. "The one who knows that pancakes are a sure way to a geek's heart."

The server dropped the check off before Katie could respond, and Abby picked it up. Katie appeared to be reaching for her pocket, but Abby shook her head.

"I've got this one."

"You sure?"

"You've been driving me around *and* you served as a tour guide. So yes. I'm sure." Abby handed the check and cash to the server when she came back then looked over at Katie. "What makes you picky about people you date?" she asked.

Katie sat back, amusement in her eyes, as if she knew Abby didn't want to discuss certain details of the dream further. "I like women of substance."

"Meaning?"

"Smart, funny, and comfortable owning both. I'm not interested in women who try to cover those up because they think that's what I'd like. Or what anyone would like. Basically, I'm not into pretenders. But geeks—that's another matter." She smiled, and Abby really wanted to pick up where they'd left off the night before.

"So what makes you old fashioned, then?"

Katie leaned forward, intent. "Stick around and find out," she said in a way that stoked a slow burn at Abby's core, the kind that made her not care about the impending geographic distance between them.

"Tempting."

"I hope so."

"I'm a sucker for temptation."

Katie grinned. "Lucky me. So would it be too forward of me to ask you out again?"

"No."

"Good. Because I'd really like to see you again."

"When?"

"Right now."

The slow burn spread down Abby's thighs. "Yes."

"How about a local history tour?"

"Oh, definitely."

Katie's grin widened and she slid out of the booth.

Stories

"THIS IS THE CLOSEST I'VE been to camping in a long time," Abby said as she stared into the flames of the fire Katie had built in a spot that, by the look of the soot-blackened stones, got used a lot. They were sitting on the ground, wrapped in a blanket.

"Hope it measures up to previous experiences." Katie's voice was low in Abby's ear, her breath warm against her skin.

Delightful chills raced up and down Abby's arms and legs. Katie sat on the ground with her back against a log, and Abby sat between Katie's legs, leaning against Katie. She stared at the fire. "It's so much better." And then she closed her eyes at the sensation of Katie's lips on her neck, and Katie's arms wrapped around her. It was like they were the only two people in the world, protected in the dark, and this clearing in the forest was all the world they needed.

"This has been the best date ever," Katie said.

"And to think it started just this morning with pancakes." She could feel the warmth of Katie's palms on her hips. One of the logs collapsed into a pile of glowing embers. She thought she heard the soft hoot of an owl in the still air. The night couldn't be any better.

"I saw you Wednesday before you went to the pub with Lu and Eleanor," Katie said after a while, nuzzling Abby's neck. "Outside the historical society."

"I know. I realized that was you waving from the SUV when we went to the glen the first night." Abby covered Katie's hands with her own. "Same SUV. Using my vast analytical skills, I figured it out."

Katie laughed softly. "But it caught me off guard, running into you again that same night."

"Almost literally."

"Mmm. And I remember thinking that there was something familiar about you, but it wasn't that I'd seen you earlier. I still don't know what that's about, but I've been feeling it since that night. And that must sound bizarre."

Abby squeezed Katie's hands. "No. Because I have that feeling, too. Since that night."

"Do you think it's strange that a Crane hooked up with a Van Tassel two hundred years after the fact?"

"And that both sets were women?"

"True," Katie said. "But it feels...right, in a way."

Abby felt Katie's smile against her neck. "I like to think that I know—at least a little—what Elizabeth felt when she met Katrina. Here she is, all dressed as a man, and she comes to this village as a school teacher. She had to have met Katrina soon after she arrived, since it wasn't that big a place and the Van Tassels were a big deal in town. I can see them having a dinner to welcome the new guy, and she walks in and there's Katrina."

"And?"

"And she can't take her eyes off her," Abby said, imagining the scene. "I'm betting Katrina was a lot like her letters. Charming, vivacious, smart. It's no wonder every guy in town was after her. Except for the smart part. Some of the guys in town probably didn't appreciate that. But then there's this new guy and Katrina finds out he really likes that she's smart, and that he talks to her like she's a person. He doesn't patronize her. He doesn't belittle her. He listens to her, and he enjoys talking to her. And maybe he sees in her a kindred spirit."

Katie laughed. "Go on." She interlaced her fingers with Abby's.

"Katrina senses it, too. She thought he was handsome, and I'll bet she thought that the first time she saw him. But she knows the ways of men, and she's had to put up with her share of assholes among them, so maybe she's a little cautious about this guy. And then he starts talking to her, and maybe she stares into his eyes because she likes how they reflect his smile, and she realizes that this guy is different. He's not an asshole. And he's warm and funny, and he laughs at her humor and appreciates what she has to say." Abby stopped, seeing the scene in her mind's eye. The dapper Ichabod Crane, dashing and handsome, delicate of feature, completely taken aback at a woman like Katrina, but totally into her. She knew what that felt like, because it had just happened to her.

"This is a really great story. Keep going." Katie wrapped her arms around Abby and pulled her even closer.

"It was that first meeting," Abby said, enjoying the warmth of Katie's embrace. "That's where Elizabeth knew that Katrina was someone special, and I'll bet as amazing as it was for her to meet Katrina, it sucked too, because she probably thought that Katrina was into guys and here Elizabeth is, not a guy, but presenting as one. But she couldn't stop coming around. She couldn't stop talking to Katrina, getting to know her. And Katrina welcomed it, though she knew her father wouldn't approve. She didn't care. And when Elizabeth revealed who she really was, I think in some ways Katrina already knew."

"Do you think Elizabeth kissed her before she revealed herself?"

"No. Maybe this is weird family loyalty, but I think Elizabeth was crazy about Katrina, but she didn't want to kiss her as a man, because that was dishonest and Katrina described Ichabod as honorable that summer she met him. I think Elizabeth revealed her secret after she was sure that Katrina could handle it. So she tells her, and I think there was this amazing moment where Katrina stares at her and then kisses her because she's so relieved. And Elizabeth makes her hot anyway and has since Katrina first saw her at that dinner." She paused. "That's where it started. The first time they met."

"How do you suppose Elizabeth became Ichabod?"

"I don't know. That's something else I have to try to figure out. But historically, women assumed male identities all the time. After all, there weren't the ID restrictions like today, so you could pretty much say you were so-and-so and nobody would question it. At least not at first. Maybe she wanted to escape a crappy marriage. Or just have more options. I have this image of her telling the family that she's going to do some mission work in Sleepy Hollow, which was perfectly acceptable for women to do, especially since there were Native peoples in the area to convert. But for whatever reason, she decided to become a school teacher."

"So she manufactures Ichabod."

"Yeah. And then when she met Katrina, she had to figure out how to make him 'real,' in a way, to preserve her own secret and deflect attention from her actual identity."

"Do you think your family knew?" Katie pressed her lips against Abby's neck and Abby sighed and pushed back into her warmth.

"They had to. At least, some of the family knew. Throughout history, there were family members of people who lived as the other gender and they kept it secret, too. Sometimes out of respect for their relative, sometimes because they considered it shameful.

"Maybe after Elizabeth and Katrina concocted this plot to get rid of Ichabod—who never really existed in the first place—the whole thing took on a life of its own. Something they couldn't have predicted. And here comes old Washington Irving and he hears about this story and all he knows is some guy named Ichabod Crane was there for a while and disappeared one night.

"And he writes the legend as he hears it. And it catches on even more." Abby stared into the flames, imagining the night Katrina masqueraded as the horseman and Elizabeth, dressed as Ichabod, disappearing and then reappearing as her actual female self. "Which means my family buried Elizabeth's other identity, too."

"Well, think about it. The story about this guy disappearing because of a ghost starts to spread, and as we both know, it changes from community to community over time. Maybe your family at the time really liked the attention, and maybe Elizabeth stirred it up." Katie's breath was warm against Abby's skin.

"Or my family just decided—especially after Irving wrote the story—that the best way to bury Ichabod was to tell people, 'yeah, we had a family member named Ichabod and he disappeared one day. We presume he's dead.' That way, nobody goes digging too much and nobody tracks it to Elizabeth. They can all say he was kind of the weird one and didn't leave any kids."

Katie hugged her a little closer. "How much do you know about your family?"

"Records are spotty in some regards, not so much in others. We can trace back to England, though. And there are several Elizabeths in the family, including in the years contemporary to Ichabod because that's not an uncommon name." She thought for a few moments. "It didn't really occur to me that the Elizabeth in Katrina's letters might be Ichabod or even remotely related to us."

"Why would it, without all the awesome circumstantial evidence we've put together?"

Abby laughed. "I've seen two specific mentions of Ichabod in some archives in Crane papers. Both said he disappeared and left no heirs. Guess I should go back and look for the name Elizabeth instead."

"That would be a really cool project."

"If we're right, and there really wasn't an Ichabod, Katrina and Elizabeth created the seeds of the legend to hide Elizabeth's secret. And they continued to see each other over the years, until Katrina died." Where did Elizabeth go, then? Definitely another mystery to track down.

Katie nuzzled her neck again. "That's sad but actually romantic."

Abby giggled. "And quite possibly not true. But I like to think that's what happened."

"So how is it that you might know what Elizabeth felt when she met Katrina?" Katie's lips moved to a spot just behind Abby's ear, which set Abby's heart to pounding much faster.

"Maybe I don't. But I do know what it feels like to meet someone special."

"I do, too."

Another log collapsed into a loose pile of embers, and Katie extricated herself from Abby and checked on the fire.

Still wrapped in the blanket, Abby joined her. "Too bad we don't have marshmallows."

Katie brushed Abby's hair out of her eyes. "I've got something else in mind," she said, running her fingertips along Abby's jawline.

Stomach flip-flopping and heart pounding, Abby leaned into her touch. Katie kissed her, and the feel of those lips sent fireworks and flares down Abby's thighs and back up again to her arms. Katie pulled her close. Their kisses deepened until Abby wasn't sure she was still standing. All she felt was Katie—her mouth, her tongue, and the solid warmth of her arms.

When Katie finally pulled away, the embers no longer glowed, and the blanket was in a heap at their feet. They were surrounded by the darkness of the forest and the distant light of a thousand stars.

"I could do that all night," Katie said, stroking Abby's cheek. "But somewhere maybe a little warmer."

Abby laughed and picked the blanket up, knowing this was a good place to stop. The chill in the air made her long for a bed and Katie wrapped around her.

Katie poured water out of a gallon jug onto the embers and then dug around in the pit with a stick. She repeated her actions, and Abby smiled, realizing Katie had brought the two jugs of water for that purpose.

"Girl Scout," Abby said.

"I'll take that as a compliment."

"It is."

Katie finished with the fire pit and kissed Abby again. A few minutes later, she stopped. "Damn," she said. "You make me really crazy, in all kinds of ways."

"I'll take that as a compliment," Abby teased.

"It is. Come on. It's pretty cold out here." She tossed the empty jugs into the back seat.

Twenty minutes later, Katie pulled up to the curb at the bed and breakfast and walked Abby to the front door again, but Abby didn't go in.

"I had the best day." Abby wished there wasn't a porch light so they could have some privacy.

"So did I. So will you have dinner with me tomorrow?"

"Absolutely." Their last night in town. Abby didn't want to think about it yet.

Katie kissed her again. "I really want to—" she stopped and held Abby's gaze. "Um. That is, I really want to get to know you better in a lot of ways. But—"

"It's not the right time or place," Abby finished. "I agree. So hold that thought." She squeezed Katie's hand.

"You're amazing." Katie brought Abby's fingertips to her lips and kissed them.

"So are you." Abby gently pulled her hand away. "Good night. I'll see you tomorrow." She went inside and Katie waved at her and blew her a kiss. Like the night before—had it only been just a day?—Abby watched her walk to her car and drive away.

She should feel totally freaked out. She should be questioning her judgment, hooking up with someone she barely knew who lived a good four hours away. But she didn't care. It felt good, it felt right, and that's what mattered. She went up to bed.

"Elizabeth."

Abby turned, relieved to hear the voice in the gloom. She felt the press of the forest around her, and the chill of the air on her face.

"We must go, love," Katrina said as she approached, her cloak drawn around her, puffs of her breath visible in the cold. She smiled and brushed Abby's hair out of her face.

And then Katrina was Katie, who grinned at her and leaned in to kiss her. "Best date ever," she said, as a big, dark horse burst into the clearing. Katie disappeared and Abby stared, unable to run or say anything.

"Elizabeth. Time to go," Katrina said from the horse's huge back. She patted the horse's rump. "He can carry us both." She reached down and Abby moved toward her and took her hand and suddenly Katrina was Katie again and Abby was on the back of the horse, her arms wrapped around Katie's waist, the horse picking up speed as Katie steered him to a path. "Hold on," Katie said, and the horse sped into a gallop, hooves pounding beneath them, the dark greens and browns of the forest flashing past. Abby held tight, Katie's back solid against her, and they burst free from the trees, into the warmth of sunlight. Abby raised one hand in the air and whooped while Katie laughed as the hoofbeats beneath kept time with an insistent beeping that soon overrode the pounding.

Abby groaned and opened her eyes. "All right," she muttered as she rolled over and shut off the alarm. Now *that* was a dream she could deal with. She went to get ready for another day of research, buoyed by the thought of dinner later with Katie and tingling from the memories of the night before.

She got to the historical society in time for coffee and donuts.

"Did you have a nice day yesterday?" Lu asked. Robert wasn't in yet, and Eleanor was sweeping out the exhibit area.

"I had a great day." Abby poured herself a cup of coffee and drank some, but the heat in her chest and down her thighs had nothing to do with the beverage.

"I hope you were able to get some sightseeing in."

Abby debated how much to say as she picked a glazed donut out of the box. "Katie actually took me on a local history tour."

"Marvelous," she said, and it sounded almost mischievous.

Abby looked at her, but Lu was reaching for a donut.

"There's quite a lot to see and do around here. I hope you had a good time."

"Oh, I did. Katie's a great tour guide." She took a bite of donut so she wouldn't say anything else.

"She is indeed. I'm glad you were both in town at the same time." Lu picked up her coffee cup. "I also made some calls to find out if anyone else had the experience you did Saturday in the glen and if anyone knows about a second horseman. I'll let you know when I find something."

"Okay. Thanks for doing that. But if it was somebody goofing off, I don't think anybody will own it. And it was a pretty good scare, so if that was the purpose, it worked."

Lu made a noncommittal noise. "Are you planning on returning for more research?"

"Definitely. Today I want to work on getting through more of Katrina's correspondence and maybe some of Baltus's. Do you know if there are other mentions of the horseman in either?"

"Yes," Eleanor said as she entered the break room. "Baltus talks about the horseman in the summer of 1800. Something to do with several sightings in the area, though he didn't personally see anything. I think Katrina mentions a sighting that fall, but it was second-hand for her, too."

"Do you know how often sightings were mentioned over the course of the Katrina and Baltus correspondences?" Abby took a second donut.

Eleanor thought for a moment. "I couldn't say, exactly, but it was more than a few times, and the sightings seemed to both attract and repel people because she mentioned visitors in the area asking questions about the phenomenon."

"Early ghost hunters," Abby said with a grin.

Lu laughed. "You might also have a look at mid to late nineteenth-century newspapers in the area, on into the twentieth century, to see how the legend evolved. Though I'm sure that's part of your research."

"Yeah, that's the second phase. I wanted to have a look at this early stuff, see what I could determine about the legends." She finished the donut. "Better get to it."

"I'll bring you the box," Lu said.

"Thanks. And thanks so much for everything."

"Always fun to have historians around who take an interest in the area."

"And when you come back, give me a call," Eleanor said. "We'd love to have you as a guest again."

"I will." Abby finished the coffee and tossed her cup into the wastebasket. She went to the reading room and set up her laptop. When Lu brought the box in, Abby got right to work. Losing herself once again in the past, she finished a couple of hours later. When she took the box back to the front counter, no one was there, but someone was in the back, so Abby waited. A few people wandered through the exhibit. She thought she heard Eleanor talking about one of the displays.

"Hi."

The voice made sparks rocket up her back. She turned toward Katie, who had just emerged from the back. "Hey," she said, smiling.

Katie wore her usual jeans, but she had a flannel shirt tucked in this time, and a white tee underneath. She'd left her hair down, and Abby longed to run her fingers through it.

"How are you?" Katie asked as she logged in the box, both on the paper form and into the computer.

"Excellent."

Katie looked up at her and smiled. "Same here. I'll go get the next box. See you in the reading room."

Abby nodded and watched her walk away before she returned to the reading room, her heart pounding amidst what felt like a full-body flush. She clearly had it bad for Katie. Really bad. And she didn't care. She held the door open for Katie, who set the box on the table and turned toward her.

Katie glanced through the door, then kissed Abby, a quick soft melding of lips that made Abby ache.

"I'm going to get sandwiches later. Can I get you one?" Katie asked, her face inches away. "It'll sort of be like having lunch together. Only with Lu, Eleanor, and probably Robert. Though I think he has a lunch thing, so maybe not Robert."

"I'd love one."

"What kind?"

"Surprise me."

Katie grinned. "It'll require that I interrupt your work. And I know how you are with Katrina."

"I think she'll understand."

"I hope so. See you in a bit. I'm going to do a couple of tours so Eleanor can take a break. Kind of busy today." She left the memory of her smile and the smell of her cologne behind, and Abby forced herself to focus on the box and the work she had to do.

At twelve-thirty, Katie reappeared. "Could you let Katrina know that your lunch is here?"

Abby looked up. "I'm hanging out with Baltus at the moment. He doesn't mind." She took the gloves off and followed Katie to the break room, remembering how it felt last night, to lose herself in Katie's kisses in the dark, miles away from anyone else.

"Oh, there you are," Lu said. Eleanor was already eating. "I have some interesting news."

"What?" Katie handed Abby a sub sandwich.

Abby unwrapped it. Turkey and Swiss. Yum.

"Well, according to all my sources, there was only one rider in the glen Saturday night."

Abby frowned. "Clearly, that wasn't the case. Somebody decided to join in. And kept it a secret, obviously, until show time."

"The society knew nothing about it," Lu added.

Katie raised her eyebrows as she unwrapped her own sandwich. "Do you actually know somebody in it?"

"I know somebody who might know somebody," Lu said with a chuckle. "Let's just say I put the word out."

"So what was the response when you asked if anybody knew whether another rider was out there?" Katie sat at the table and Abby sat next to her.

"Confused. Apparently, it's never happened before, at least not that anybody remembers. And it's not society policy, because two riders could cause problems."

"It's true," Katie said. "That one sure did."

"What did the rider look like, again?" Lu asked.

"Big black horse," Abby said. "The rider was dressed in dark clothing. Sword on his—uh—right side, I think. And there was something brass. Like buttons on a coat. He had some kind of coat on, maybe." She went back to that night and remembered how the horse had jumped over her, no sound. No smell. Nothing. "You know what was weird? I didn't hear anything. I mean, besides the hoofbeats."

Katie stopped chewing. "Yeah. I heard those, too. But none of the usual horse and rider sounds." She caught Abby's gaze and Abby saw her own thoughts mirrored in Katie's eyes.

"You don't think—" Abby started.

"I'm not sure what to think."

"Where were you when you saw this rider?" Lu asked.

"That one path north of the place where ghost hunters normally park," Katie said. "About a mile in. We started at that little bypass just off the main route because the society horseman normally takes it. And he did. So then we went out onto the main road and then we walked north to that path so we could take it across the glen, since we parked on the other side. The regular horseman usually goes south, to the periphery, and that's where we heard cheers coming from."

"Let me make a call," Lu said. "Maybe I wasn't specific enough."

She left and Katie gave Abby a wide-eyed look. Eleanor's cell phone rang. She answered and took the call out of the break room, leaving Katie and Abby alone.

"Some things are beyond science," Katie said.

"I know, but really? A ghost?"

"Somebody back in the day saw something, and that's what started this whole legend thing. Whether it was a ghost or something the person thought was a ghost isn't really the issue. Either way, a legend was born."

"And you called him a dick." Abby laughed. "Do you think if he was a ghost, he knew what that meant?"

"Had I known we were possibly dealing with a dead guy over two hundred years old, I guess I could have said something like, 'verily, you, sir, are the son of a sow.' Though 'asshole' is enough like 'arsehole' that he might have understood that. Assuming he spoke enough English in life."

"But then there's the matter of his head. He probably wouldn't have heard you no matter what you called him."

Katie laughed. "I hope the horse spoke English, then. And regardless, ghost or not, he was a dick."

Abby smiled. "That is totally based on scientific observation." She caught Katie's gaze and neither spoke for a few moments.

Katie broke the silence. "I really want to kiss you."

Again, Abby understood what "swoon" meant. She was about to reply when Lu returned.

"Well," Lu said, "the annual horseman doesn't ride that route and has never ridden that route because it's safer on the southern periphery and gives the best chance of visibility." She looked first at Katie and then at Abby. "However, historically speaking, the northern area of the glen has many recorded sightings of the actual horseman."

"So could it have been somebody who's not from this area?" Abby asked.

"Seems it would be kind of hard to pull off that kind of prank if you're not from the area," Katie said. "If you don't know the glen, you'll have a hard time racing at top speed along those paths. Especially if your horse hasn't done it."

"And there's no chance it was a local playing a prank?"

"Of course there's a chance of that, but what would be the point, given that most of the spectators are to the south?" Lu sat down again. "It seems that if you want your prank to have an impact, you want lots of people to see it."

"So you're basically saying that there is a distinct possibility that we saw the actual horseman." Katie fiddled with the wrapper her sandwich had come in.

"It would seem that way," Lu said.

"As much as I don't want to believe it, there are only two options. Ghost or prank. And so far, prank doesn't make much sense." Abby looked at Katie.

"Damn," Katie said softly and Abby remembered how the horseman had seemingly just appeared from the darkness, without much warning.

"Would you like to log an official sighting?" Lu asked with a smile. "Because your experience involved a lot more than many."

"No," both Katie and Abby responded.

"We don't have proof," Abby added. "Because there is still a chance it was a second human rider."

"Though circumstantial evidence suggests otherwise." Katie smiled at Lu. "Let's just make it part of family lore."

"I'd like that, too." Abby smiled. "Family lore." She thought about the dreams she'd had every night in Sleepy Hollow, and how they seemed to be both messages and reflections. Some things were definitely beyond science.

"All right." Lu looked at Katie. "Can you handle a couple more tours this afternoon?"

"Yep."

"Great. Ten minutes." Lu threw her sandwich wrapper away and took her drink with her.

"What do you think?" Katie asked after Lu had left.

"I'm leaning ghost."

"Same here. But I'm not sure why. Maybe because I want it that way."

"Isn't that part of legends? People need them in a way, to help identify with something, whether it's a place or something else."

Katie took her hand. "I like that we have a story to add to the legend. Speaking of, are you going to include our theories about Elizabeth and Katrina in your dissertation?"

"I don't know. I thought about it, but then I wondered if it would ruin the rest of the legend."

"But it could start whole new ones. And the horseman doesn't need a shift in gender perceptions to ride. There'll always be a festival, and there'll always be sightings of a ghost. A change in Ichabod's story isn't necessarily going to change that."

"I guess I could address it that way, and include it as a 'what if' sort of thing, and what it might mean in the context of a much older folklore." Abby liked that approach, because it left room for conjecture, and the development of new stories to layer into the older without uprooting the latter.

"Exactly." Katie ran her thumb over the back of Abby's fingers. "So how about I pick you up at six?"

"Definitely."

"Great. Okay, off I go." She released Abby's hand and cleared the table as she left.

Abby finished her iced tea and went back to the reading room, thinking about stories and the events behind them. And she thought, too, about the coincidence of a Crane meeting a Van Tassel so many years later. Or was it a coincidence? *You're part of the legend, now,* Eleanor had said. Maybe she was. And maybe Elizabeth and Katrina would finally rest. She pulled another file out of the box.

Katie pulled up in front of the bed and breakfast and put her car in park. "This has been an amazing few days." She took Abby's hand.

"I agree." Abby wished dinner hadn't ended, wished neither of them was going back to their respective universities the next morning. She lifted Abby's hand to her lips and kissed it. "I want to keep seeing you," she said against Abby's skin. "Is that possible?"

Chills shot up Abby's spine at Katie's touch. "Will it involve dressing up as a headless horseman to create a diversion?"

"Not unless you're into that. But hey, I'll roll with it."

Abby laughed. "All in good time." Katie's lips made her tingle in all kinds of places.

"Is that a yes?"

"Yes. I mean, yes, it is a yes and yes. To the other thing. Yes all around."

Katie leaned in and kissed her, and Abby lost herself again in the feel of her lips and tongue and how she tasted like coffee from the cup they'd shared with dessert at the restaurant.

"I have to stop," Katie said after a few delicious moments. "Because if I don't, I won't be able to."

"You do have a back seat," Abby teased.

"True. But we're not in high school."

Abby gave her another long, lingering kiss. "I don't know. You kind of make me feel that way." And right now, she would totally get into the back seat with Katie and fog up the windows.

"Is that a good thing?"

"Very." Abby gave her another kiss.

"When can I see you again?" Katie asked. "In real life. Not just FaceTime or Skype."

"The weekend before Thanksgiving?"

"Done. I'll check to make sure. How about I come to Connecticut?"

"I would really like that."

"Same here. And now, I really need for us to get out of this car before I do invite you into the back seat."

"Which might be memorable," Abby said as she opened the car door.

"I have no doubt. But I'm being responsible, here. We both have to drive in the morning." Katie walked her to the front door of the bed and breakfast, a habit Abby enjoyed. She glanced into the building's interior to see if any of the other guests were up walking around or hanging out in the front room, but it was late enough that they weren't.

She pulled Katie into a hug. "I don't know why, but I feel really connected to you," she said softly near Katie's ear.

"Talk to you later." She pulled away trying to be responsible, too, but oh, it was hard. She unlocked the door, went inside and turned to wave at Katie through the glass. Katie blew her a kiss before returning to her car, and Abby watched as she drove away from the curb. Damn. Should've taken her into the back seat, maybe. She went up the stairs to her room, still tingling, still aching, wishing for Katie's company.

Abby threw her sweatshirt onto her suitcase, kicked her shoes off, and flopped onto the bed, Katie's cologne still somehow lingering on her T-shirt. Her phone rang with Katie's tone. She rolled over and retrieved it from the bedside table.

"Hey," Abby said. "What's up?"

"I decided I don't want to be responsible tonight."

Abby's heartbeat sped up. "Good. What does that entail?"

"Letting me in. I'm downstairs."

"I'll be right there." Abby didn't bother putting her shoes back on. She practically raced down the stairs to the front door. "Hi again," she said when she opened the door.

"Hi." Katie smiled and stepped inside. She pulled Abby close and kissed her in a way that made crazy little bombs explode up and down Abby's back and made heat pool between her legs.

When Katie finally stopped, Abby barely remembered to close and lock the door. She took Katie's hand and guided her upstairs to her room.

Katie closed the door behind them. "I didn't want to leave tomorrow without seeing you."

"We could've met for breakfast," Abby said as she pushed Katie's coat off her shoulders.

Katie shrugged out of it and tossed it onto a nearby chair.

She wrapped her arms around Abby. "Not the same thing." Katie pressed her lips against Abby's neck.

Oh, how Abby loved that. She buried her fingers in Katie's hair and closed her eyes as Katie's lips worked their way to Abby's ear and then back down to her skin just above the collar of her T-shirt.

Katie had one hand on Abby's hip, and the other cupped Abby's cheek as Katie's mouth met Abby's. Katie kissed her hard and deep, until Abby wasn't sure she was still standing because she couldn't feel her feet on the floor. Abby worked her hands down to the hem of Katie's sweatshirt, and she slid her hands underneath it and Katie's tee. Her fingertips met the warmth of Katie's skin just above her jeans.

Katie's breathing sped up against Abby's lips. She stopped kissing Abby for a moment and started to pull her sweatshirt off, leaving her T-shirt in place. Abby helped and tossed it aside. She felt Katie's hands moving under her shirt, Katie's fingertips gliding over her skin, and pinpricks of pleasure danced down Abby's legs.

Abby withdrew her hands, but only to start taking her shirt off. She tore it off, impatient, and Katie took hers off, too, and dropped it on the floor next to Abby's.

Katie stared at her and ran her fingers across Abby's bare shoulders then down her arms. A mixture of chills and heat made Abby tremble, and the look in Katie's eyes made her breath catch.

"You're gorgeous." Katie leaned down and kissed the bare skin above Abby's bra.

Abby ran her hands down Katie's back, and she wanted much more of Katie against her body, without the barrier of clothing. Her fingers brushed Katie's belt, and she worked them around to the front of her jeans and tugged at it.

Katie's fingers moved between Abby's as they fumbled with the belt, her breath hard and fast against Abby's mouth. "I was worried you'd think I was a little too forward, showing up like this," Katie said. "But clearly, I didn't need to."

Abby smiled as she finished unclasping Katie's belt and then unbuttoned her jeans. "No, you didn't." She guided Katie's hands to the button on her own jeans, and while Katie was occupied with that, Abby unclasped her bra and let it slip off her shoulders.

Katie's hands moved up Abby's stomach, to stop right below her breasts. "Do you even know the effect you have on me?" she whispered as she ran her fingertips lightly over Abby's nipples and what felt like an electrical jolt raced through Abby's core.

"If it's anything like the one you have on me, then I can guess," Abby managed as she encouraged Katie's hands to cup her breasts. "Oh, God," she said with a gasp. And then she wasn't quite sure how Katie managed to remove her own bra, but she did and pulled Abby against her, and the heat from Katie's skin against her own tore a soft groan from Abby.

Katie backed her against the bed, and they fell together onto the covers. With a smile, Katie leaned down and kissed her.

Abby caressed Katie's breasts, and her nipples hardened against Abby's palms. She pulled her mouth away from Katie's and ran her tongue lightly over each of Katie's nipples, then pulled one hard into her mouth while she gently squeezed the other, eliciting a gasp from Katie. Abby's free hand slid down Katie's back and she brushed her fingertips just underneath Katie's underwear, accessible now that her jeans were loosened.

"I need you out of these," Abby said around Katie's nipple as she pushed at Katie's jeans with her free hand.

Katie obliged, bracing herself on one hand while she kicked her shoes off then worked her jeans down her thighs, though she left her underwear on. And then she pressed the length of her body against Abby, kissing her hard for a few moments. She stopped and straddled Abby's hips and pinned Abby's hands on the bed above her head, their fingers entwined. Katie stared into Abby's eyes before leaning down and unleashing a delicious assault on Abby's mouth with her own, her breasts brushing Abby's with her motions. Abby moaned against Katie's lips and surrendered to her ministrations, burning in places she didn't know she had.

Katie stopped, breathing hard. "I really want to take your pants off."

"God, yes."

Katie laughed, low in her throat, and released Abby's hands so she could help until there was nothing between them but their underwear. Katie's thighs against Abby's brought another jolt of heat and moisture to Abby's core and the throbbing between her legs increased until she was sure that all Katie had to do was touch her and she'd come. As if she'd read her mind, Katie ran her fingertips lightly back and forth over the front of Abby's underwear. Gasping, Abby automatically moved against Katie's hand.

"I need to feel you." Katie slid Abby's panties off.

Abby reached for Katie's but she was already taking those off, too, and then Abby lost herself in Katie's hands and lips and the way her skin slid against hers. And when Katie finally entered her, Abby cried out at the feel of Katie's fingers. She held on as waves of sensation rocketed through her until she crested and fell back to earth, trembling from aftershocks and something else she couldn't name.

"I've got you," Katie said softly as she pulled Abby close and Abby almost cried. She kissed Katie, a tender meeting of lips that intensified quickly until Katie moaned, and Abby repositioned herself so that Katie was underneath her, and she moved her hand to Katie's damp heat. Whimpering as Abby stroked her, Katie welcomed her fingers with a groan and wrapped her legs around Abby, moving with her tentatively at first and then with greater urgency. Abby matched her rhythm and increased her thrusts until Katie released with a long, low moan and fell back onto the bed, panting and shuddering.

Abby gathered her in her arms and ran her fingers idly through Katie's hair, hoping this wasn't another dream.

"You are so completely amazing." Katie repositioned herself and looked into Abby's eyes. "I'm so glad you didn't want to be responsible tonight."

"We may yet have to. Eleanor is usually up pretty early."

Katie grinned. "And she'll see me leaving if I stay." She leaned in and kissed Abby. "I don't care."

"I could tell her we were doing research. Maybe testing some theories." Abby ran her thumb over Katie's lips.

"And I was so exhausted afterward that I just stayed." Katie nipped at Abby's thumb. "Yeah, that's totally legit. She'll buy that."

Abby giggled. "Just trying to help."

"And I appreciate it. But the fact is, I only care about being here with you." She caressed Abby's face. "And doing that every chance I get."

"You sure know how to get a girl all worked up." Abby ran her hand along Katie's arm to her hand, which she took in her own.

"I'm only interested in getting one in particular worked up." She smiled. "As long as I possibly can." She moved, then, until she ended up on top of Abby, staring into her eyes. "I don't know what's going to happen, but I do know that there's something between us and I want to keep exploring it."

"Same here," Abby said, Katie's words coursing like electricity through her body. She pulled Katie against her and kissed her. "Let's do that now."

Katie grinned. "Good idea," she said as she nuzzled Abby's neck. "I'll start."

Abby closed her eyes and let her.

Dreams

ABBY PULLED INTO A PARKING space almost as close to the historical society as the first time she'd come to Sleepy Hollow, nearly two months ago. Strange, but it was like coming home. Did Elizabeth feel that way when she came to Sleepy Hollow? Like it was home in some way and a place she belonged? Abby had taken to thinking of Ichabod as Elizabeth, though she and Katie hadn't definitively proven their theory. Some things just felt right, and seeing the legend with that perspective was one of the things that did.

She grabbed the tote bag of gifts from the passenger seat and got out, stepping carefully in the slush underfoot. Since she was only a few yards from where she was going, she didn't bother with her winter jacket. Her sweatshirt would be fine for the short trip inside.

The trees no longer bore their autumn finery and instead stood dark and leafless, a thin blanket of late December snow spread across many branches. More snow was due, Abby could tell from the slate sky and the chill in the air. She locked her car and walked carefully to the sidewalk. Christmas banners had replaced the Halloween, advertising a holiday festival in the next couple of days. The city lampposts were wrapped in red, green, and gold tinsel and some enterprising soul across the street had decorated several tree trunks with red lights. She smiled and wondered if Katrina and Elizabeth had ever been able to spend a Christmas together.

Abby stamped her feet on the thick rubber mat outside the historical society before she went in, where she wiped her feet on the mat inside. The doorbell sounded and Lu emerged from the back.

"Well, hi." Lu came around the counter and gave Abby a hug. "It's so good to see you. And I have a lead on some papers in Boston I think you might want to see."

"That's excellent. Load me up. Research rocks."

Lu laughed. "How about after Christmas?"

"That'll work." Abby set her bag on the floor and took three small wrapped packages out that she placed on the counter. "Happy holidays," she said as she handed one to Lu. "You can open it now."

"And ruin the surprise before Christmas Eve? I can wait until tomorrow."

"These are for Eleanor and Robert." Abby gestured at the other two packages.

"How sweet of you. They're both gone for the day, so. I'll put these in the back." Lu took all three and returned a few moments later. "How was the drive?"

"Slow. Lots of traffic, but the weather wasn't too bad."

"Not yet. We're supposed to get a good storm tonight and tomorrow." Lu shrugged. "That time of year." She smiled, sly. "Have you called Katie yet?"

"Yes. I told her I would be stopping here first." She was relieved that she didn't blush.

Lu started to say something but the door opened and a woman came in, wearing a blue lightweight winter coat, headband and gray trousers. She wiped her shoes on the mat.

"Lu," she said, "I need you to pick up the turkey—" she stopped when she saw Abby. "Hi. My wild guess is that you must be Abby." She grinned.

"Uh, yes."

"I'm Rachel. Lu's sister." She pulled her glove off and held out her hand. "Katie's mom."

"Oh, wow. Hi. I'm so glad to finally meet you." Abby shook Rachel's hand, glad that Rachel had a strong, comfortable grip. And now that Abby looked at her, she could see the resemblance not only to Lu, but Katie. She should have been more nervous, but she wasn't. It felt entirely comfortable, meeting Rachel like this without Katie as a buffer.

"And I am glad to finally meet you. Katie talks quite a bit about you."

Lu laughed. "Nonstop."

This time Abby blushed, which made Rachel laugh. "It's so nice to have you here for Christmas. I wish we had the room to put you up, but we've got Katie and her brother and sister in town and my other sister is coming tonight with her family."

"That's okay. The holidays are crazy like that. Eleanor saved my room for me." Abby liked Rachel's welcoming and down-to-earth vibe. Katie had said that her parents were accepting of her, and for that Abby would be ever grateful.

"My son is leaving Christmas Day," Lu said. "You're welcome to his guest room at my place when he does."

"That's a great offer, but—"

"Oh, take it." Rachel took her other glove off and shoved both into her coat pocket. "Katie would insist, and I'm insisting now. Might as well get a good seat for the spectacle of this family gathering for Christmas. Besides, Lu and I both know what grad student budgets are all about."

"Okay. I'll let Eleanor know. Thanks so much."

"Absolutely," Rachel said. "And before I forget, Lu, could you pick up the turkey tomorrow? I already paid for it. I'll get it when we come over tomorrow evening."

Lu wrote something on a sticky note pad on the counter. "What time are we eating on Christmas Day?"

"Four. Do you need anything else for tomorrow?"

Lu stopped writing. "I think we're covered. Abby, is there anything in terms of food or drink that you'd like? Or anything you can't have?"

"Whatever you have is fine. I don't have any dietary restrictions."

"Lucky." Rachel mock-sighed. "Then we'll be over tomorrow around five." To Abby she said, "I'm sure Katie's already told you, but we have a gathering Christmas Eve and open presents then. That way we all get to sleep in on Christmas Day and be lazy until we have dinner."

"She did mention that." Abby smiled. "Looking forward to both Christmas Eve and Christmas Day."

"What about your folks?" Lu asked.

Abby looked at her. "My parents took a cruise for Christmas. My sisters and I got it for them. So we already opened our gifts and had our holiday gathering."

"Then you get two Christmases. And we're very glad one of them is with us." Lu put the note she'd been writing into the pocket of her flannel shirt.

"See you in a bit." Rachel had just begun to put her gloves on when Katie burst in, grinning like she'd just won the lottery.

She wore a thick cream-colored sweater under her barn jacket, which she hadn't bothered to button, and her faded jeans bunched at the tops of her hikers. She looked like a co-ed lumberjack, and Abby adored her for it.

"Hey—" Katie started. "Oh, damn. I wanted to introduce you to my mom."

"We managed." Rachel smiled at Abby, then back at Katie.

"Oh, Rachel, I need your opinion about something." Lu motioned toward the back and Rachel went around the counter and followed her, wearing the same sly smile that Lu had.

Katie pulled Abby into a hug as soon as Rachel and Lu left. "I missed you. Bad."

Abby held on tight. "Same here." She hadn't seen Katie in the flesh since the weekend before Thanksgiving at UConn. FaceTime and Skype just didn't do her justice.

Before Abby could say anything else, Katie kissed her, and it made her nerve endings smolder. Sparks shot up Abby's back and she wondered if they were visible, floating above her head.

Katie pulled away first. "I could do that all day."

"I'd let you."

Katie smiled and caressed Abby's cheek. "How was the drive?"

"Traffic, so it was slow. But it doesn't matter because I'm here."

"Have you had dinner?"

"No."

"Me, either. So how about we go get some and then I'll take you to my folks' house so you can meet a few more members of my crazy family?"

Abby leaned into Katie's hand, still on her cheek. "Sounds great. Let me drop my stuff off at Eleanor's and then we can go wherever you want."

"Okay, I'll see you tomorrow," Lu said to Rachel as they emerged from the back.

Katie pulled her hand away from Abby's face, and grabbed Abby's hand instead.

Lu saw and smiled.

"We're going to get some dinner and then we'll be over after that." Katie pecked Rachel on the cheek.

"Good. Abby should probably be well-fortified before she meets more of us." Rachel gave Abby's shoulder a squeeze. "See you soon."

Katie pulled Abby toward the door, opened it, and walked Abby to her car. "I'll follow you to Eleanor's. Is it okay if I drive you around while you're here?"

"I was hoping you would, since you're my local tour guide."

"Seems you fit in pretty well already." Katie kissed her again, which warmed Abby up a lot faster than the heater in her car would. "See you there."

Twenty minutes later, Abby was checked in at the bed and breakfast and buckling up in Katie's SUV. Katie didn't start the engine right away. Instead, she leaned over and kissed Abby, and this time she didn't stop, not for what seemed like a long time, and Abby was sure the heat she felt would melt the snow outside the vehicle if she opened the door.

"We'll never make it to your parents' house at this rate," Abby said against Katie's lips.

"True. And then my brother will tease the shit out of me for months." She groaned softly and pulled away. "Okay. Let's go. We must keep up our strength."

"Definitely. And not just for your family."

"Saying things like that doesn't make me want to get dinner."

"Hold that thought for later."

Katie groaned again and drove away from the curb.

Clearly, New England reserve was not something Katie's family was acquainted with, because the moment Abby stepped into Katie's parents' house—a big, rambling Victorian—she was surrounded by laughter and good-natured teasing. Katie's older sister Krista was married to a man, and they had brought their two young children. Katie's brother Thad was a year younger than Katie, but he had come alone because his girlfriend was in California with her family. Tom, Katie's dad, was a tall athletic guy with curly blond hair and a booming voice that would have made a lot of preachers jealous.

Katie's aunt was almost as loud as her teen daughter, but they were drowned out when a few friends of Thad's stopped by at one point, and two of them started reminiscing about high school with Thad and Katie. Abby slipped away to the kitchen for something to drink and for a few moments of quiet.

Rachel and Tom had spent a lot of time and money on refurbishing the house. It retained many of its original touches, but they'd updated all the windows, electrical, and plumbing. They'd also created a modern space in the kitchen, which looked like something you might see in a culinary magazine, with its urban chic appliances, tile floor, and granite countertops.

Abby got a Diet Coke from the refrigerator and stood sipping it, listening to the laughter from the other room. She picked Katie's voice out of the crowd and smiled as warmth spread through her chest at the sound of it.

"Everything okay?"

Abby looked up as Krista came in. She was tall, like her dad, but her hair was the same dark color as Katie's and Rachel's. She wore jeans and a baggy red sweater.

"Fine. Just needed something to drink." Abby moved so Krista could open the fridge. She retrieved a Diet Coke, too.

"I know. We're a little loud. We don't take it personally if you need to hide in the kitchen for a few minutes. Plus, meeting the girlfriend's family is always stressful."

Girlfriend. Katie had been referring to her that way with her family. That made Abby's night even better than it was, though it was really good so far. "Maybe a little stressful. But I've been looking forward to it."

"Poor thing. You have no idea." She opened her can of soda. "Katie tells us you have two sisters."

Abby smiled. Katie had indeed been talking her up. "Yes. One's younger than me, the other's older. We got our parents a cruise for Christmas. So that's where the folks are. We celebrated Christmas early this year."

"What a great idea." She took a drink just as Katie entered the kitchen.

"There you are." Katie took Abby's hand.

"Two little lovers, sittin' in a tree," Thad chanted from the doorway.

Katie rolled her eyes. "Really? How old are we?"

He laughed and moved away.

"I told Krista about our possible encounter with the horseman," Katie said.

Abby looked at Krista, who took another sip of her soda before she spoke.

"Sounds like an honest-to-god sighting of the Hollow's favorite Hessian." Krista half-shrugged. "This is one of those places where strange things happen all the time. Exciting, though, that you both saw him at the same time."

"Did she tell you some of our other theories?" Abby squeezed Katie's hand.

"A bit. I like them. Katie's the one who's most obsessed with the history of this area. Well, her and Lu. Do you plan on doing anything with those ideas?"

"We've been talking about writing a paper together." Katie let go of Abby's hand and instead put her arm around Abby's waist. Abby loved that she did that, here in her parents' house. Her own parents were accepting, but a little more uptight than Katie's family. Maybe they'd loosen up a bit, with Katie around. It was hard not to relax and have fun with her.

Krista laughed. "You grad student types and your papers."

"Well, yeah. Somebody has to write them." Katie kissed Abby on the cheek.

"It's really nice to meet you," Krista said to Abby. "We're glad you're here." A child started crying and she sighed. "That's my cue. Time to put someone to bed. If I don't see you again tonight, we'll see you tomorrow at Lu's."

"Yes. Looking forward to it," Abby replied.

Krista left and Katie once again took Abby's hand. "How are you holding up? We're kind of a loud bunch."

"Krista said the same thing." Abby slid her arms around Katie's waist and rested her head against her shoulder. "But I'm enjoying it."

"Are you tired? Long drive and then this motley crew could wear out the strongest among us."

"Yes. But I really like where I am right now." Abby closed her eyes and enjoyed the feel of Katie's embrace, and the solidity of her body. Yep, she could definitely stay right here for a long time.

"Same here. But in the interest of getting more alone time with you, how about I drive you back to Eleanor's? I'm hoping you'll want my company after we get there, of course."

"Funny." Abby moved so she could see Katie's face. "I was just trying to figure out how to talk you into spending the night with me."

Katie's eyes widened. "It won't be hard."

"I hope not. Because I really missed you."

Katie held Abby's gaze, something warm and deep in her eyes, and again Abby had the sense that she was home, that she belonged here.

"Are you ready to go, then?" Katie asked.

"Not to be rude to your family, but yes." She gently pulled Katie out of the kitchen, and once they were back among the others, Katie took the lead and expertly maneuvered Abby to the front door.

"I'll go get our coats." Katie turned, but Rachel appeared.

"Here they are." Rachel held the coats up.

"Thanks." Abby put hers on. "And thanks so much for your hospitality."

Rachel smiled. "It's good to have you here."

Katie put her coat on and buttoned it. "I'm going to drive Abby back to Eleanor's."

"Then we'll see you both tomorrow." Rachel gave her a wicked smile. "But I can't be responsible for anything your brother says to you."

Katie said something under her breath that Abby didn't catch, but Rachel did because she laughed. Abby smiled, in spite of her blush.

"Good night, you two."

"Good night, Mom."

"'Night." Abby opened the front door and stepped out onto the big porch into the cold, Katie right behind her. They stepped off the porch onto the walk.

"Look." Abby pointed at the sky. "It's snowing. Does the horseman make appearances this time of year?"

"Yes, according to accounts. Why?"

"We could look for tracks in the glen. Horseman plus tracks equals human. Horseman plus no tracks equals something else entirely."

"I like it. Science."

Abby shrugged. "Maybe. Maybe not. And maybe I just want to get you alone there."

"I like it even more. We'll test this theory tomorrow, weather permitting. Did you bring all your snow clothes?"

"Yes. Since I'm with a Girl Scout, I figured I should probably get with it."

Katie ran her fingers along Katie's jaw, cupped her cheek, and kissed her. "I really like this story," she said. "I want to see what we do with it."

"Me, too."

"Good. So how about you start talking me into spending the night with you?"

"I was hoping there wouldn't be much talk involved."

"I knew I liked you." Katie opened the car door for her.

Snow clung to Abby's clothing and she smelled wet wool and wood smoke. Voices drifted toward her through the dark, punctuated by laughter and what might have been singing, though it was completely off-key. All around her the trees stood silent in their winter cloaks. Several lights glowed beyond the trunks of the closest trees, but they didn't seem to move. Houses, maybe?

Abby took a step, watching where she put her feet in the snow and she stopped, confused. Why was she wearing a skirt? She touched her thighs. Not just one skirt. An outer, heavy one beneath which she determined was at least one other of a lighter weight. And was this a coat she wore? No, it was a dark woolen cloak, heavy anyway, but with the added moisture from the snow, it hung on her shoulders, a limp weight that made it difficult to maneuver. Beneath the cloak she wore a vest or jerkin of some sort and a coarse blouse beneath that.

Annoying, that she wasn't in trousers, but she resumed taking careful steps toward the lights because she sensed she needed to, though wet cold had seeped into her shoes. The forest seemed to part, providing an unfettered view of several wooden houses. Smoke curled from each chimney. A cloaked figure on a big black horse approached, but Abby wasn't afraid. She waited.

"Elizabeth," the figure said as she reined the horse to a stop, and it stood, puffs of its breath mingling with the snow.

The voice sent a thrill from Abby's chest to her thighs. "Yes."

Katrina dismounted and the horse seemed to dissolve in a flurry of dark snowflakes that mixed with the white. "My love, come inside. Even the Hessian wouldn't ride in this." Her tone was teasing and then Katrina was close enough to touch, and she wasn't Katrina, but Katie.

She reached out and arranged the hood of Abby's cloak so that it covered her head. "I've made up the bed," Katie said. "Now please come with me and warm up."

Abby let Katie take her hand, surprised at its warmth, and suddenly they stood at the door of one of the larger houses. Dim light glowed through the windows, casting half of Katie's face in shadow.

"I've missed you." Katie cupped Abby's face with both hands. "And you found your way back." She kissed Abby, a slow, gentle meeting of lips.

The distant sound of hoofbeats matched the pounding of Abby's heart, until they were so loud that she turned from Katie toward the forest, seeing nothing but the snow and the dark shapes of the trees through the eerie winter light and heard nothing but silence and voices from a neighboring house.

Katie's arms encircled her from behind and Abby sighed, contented.

"Elizabeth," Katie said softly in her ear.

Abby's eyes snapped open. She was on her side in bed, facing one of the shuttered windows. Katie was spooning her, one arm holding her close.

"You're home," a woman's voice whispered.

Abby held her breath, listening, because that wasn't Katie.

"Mmm." Katie stirred and pulled her closer. "What?" she asked, voice thick with sleep.

"Did you hear something?" Abby kept her voice low.

"Thought you said something."

"It wasn't me."

Katie went totally still and Abby knew she was listening, too. The seconds crawled past and finally, Katie sat up in the bed and turned the bedside light on. Abby blinked and covered her eyes for a couple of seconds before she moved her hand and watched as Katie got out of bed and checked the door, which was clearly still locked. Katie also checked the bathroom and then under the bed, which made Abby giggle nervously.

"Nothing." She got back into bed and Abby wrapped her in a hug. Katie's skin was cool from being out of the warmth of the covers.

"Well, if there *was* something, it got an eyeful."

Katie laughed. "There's no naked ghost hunter show?"

"No, fortunately." Abby snuggled closer. "And why are you talking about ghosts?"

"Because that was weird. Though I'm willing to concede that I was mostly asleep and could have dreamed it."

"I did dream. And then I was awake and heard something."

"You dreamed?"

Abby gave her the rundown. "You called me Elizabeth. In my dream. I woke up and thought maybe you were talking in your sleep. But it didn't sound like you."

"Do you think you could have said something? In the interest of scientific inquiry, after all. We have to consider all possibilities before we go the way of the ghost hunter."

"I suppose I could have. I thought I was fully awake, but maybe I wasn't."

"Could somebody have said something in the hallway as they walked past?"

Abby moved so she could see the bedside clock on her side. "At almost two-thirty in the morning? Eleanor might have a fit if people were walking through the halls talking at this hour." She turned back to Katie.

"True."

"It was probably me. You thought I said something, after all. I just thought I was awake and sometimes, I do talk in my sleep." She relaxed more. That was most likely the case. Who knew why dreams might cause you to say weird things in your sleep?

"Which isn't uncommon. So there is a possibility that you said something." Katie was quiet for a while, but her hands were busy, roaming across Abby's back and down her arms. "So I was Katrina," she said, drawing designs along her spine and making Abby sigh with pleasure.

"And I was Elizabeth. It was a dream," Abby said. "Crazy things happen in dreams."

"Do you have dreams like that when you're not in Sleepy Hollow?"

"No. And I'd like them to stop." But she didn't want Katie's hands to stop.

Katie's fingers continued tracing lines on Abby's skin, much to Abby's approval. "I said in the dream that you found your way back. Well, the Katrina me said that, right?"

"Yes." Abby nuzzled Katie's neck.

"So maybe that was it."

"What do you mean?"

"The last dream."

"Why?" Abby positioned herself so she could look at Katie.

"Well, here you are, a Crane, back in Sleepy Hollow."

Abby smiled. "Seduced by a Van Tassel. You're suggesting it's a full circle kind of thing?"

"Maybe. And wait. I seduced you?" Katie raised her eyebrows. "I seem to recall you kissed me first."

"You gave me plenty of incentive."

"Guilty. Here's some more." Katie pulled her close and Abby lost herself in how Katie's lips felt against hers, and heat built at her core.

"That definitely works," Abby said.

Katie stopped and moved like she was going to turn the light off.

"No." Abby pulled her back. "Leave it on."

"Okay. Where were we?"

"Right here." And Abby kissed her again.

How different the glen looked this time of year, Abby thought as she and Katie walked the path they'd been on the night they saw the second horseman. The trees seemed almost forlorn without their leaves, the snow on their limbs somehow accentuating that instead of hiding it.

Others had been out already. No surprise, since it was early afternoon. Various tracks—including those of skis—had marked the path though the two of them still had to walk single-file. Overhead, a sullen gray sky portended more snow, and the air carried the cold metallic smell of winter. Abby didn't care. Normally not a fan of the season, she was enjoying it this year more than she ever had, and every time she thought about last night with Katie—or Katie in general—everything tingled.

"I'd say this is about the right spot," Katie stopped and turned to face Abby. "The initial sighting of the asshole horseman."

Abby looked around. She wouldn't have known it even if the trees were leafed out. It had been dark then, as well. "How do you even know that?"

"I timed the walk. This is the vicinity, give or take a few yards. That whole Girl Scout thing I have going on."

Abby grabbed the front of Katie's coat and pulled her close for a kiss that turned into several more. "That's for that night," Abby said as she let go of her coat. "Because that's what I wanted to do right before he showed up."

"Me, too." Katie grinned. "But I'm glad you didn't, because it would have been interrupted."

"Yeah. He totally ruined the moment."

"At least in that respect."

They stood in silence, holding hands and listening. The wind sounded different in winter. Clearer, like it had a sharp edge, and noise carried better. Someone shouted something, and Abby guessed the person was a quarter-mile away.

"I don't see any horse tracks," Katie said.

"Do people ride here in the winter?" Abby peered down the path behind Katie, scrutinizing the track patterns.

"Quite a bit. Doesn't look like anybody's out with their horses today, though. Probably tomorrow, since everything will be closed for Christmas Day."

"Shh." Abby placed a gloved finger against Katie's lips and they both listened again, but all she heard was the wind, distant voices, and Katie breathing. "Does he not ride during the day?"

"Historically, people have recorded daytime sightings." Katie kissed the tip of Abby's nose. "Maybe he's resigned to the fact that a Crane is back in the glen and she figured out the mystery. He can't put one over on you."

"Or maybe it was just a human asshole."

"Maybe." Katie's tone didn't suggest that she believed that, though. Abby didn't, either. She leaned against Katie, who wrapped her in an embrace.

"I know that you do your big gift-giving extravaganza tonight at Lu's—" Abby started.

"Not really." Katie smiled. "The kids get most of the gifts. The adults usually just exchange one or two. Otherwise, it'd be out of control and some kind of crazy capitalist frenzy. We prefer to just have big parties, for the most part."

"And I like that. But my point is, I'd like to give mine to you now."

"Does it involve more time with you?"

"Yes."

"Then I'm all about early gift-giving." Katie put her hands on Abby's hips.

"Good. First, I got the grant."

"Oh, my God, that's—wow. Congratulations." Katie grinned and pulled her close again. "When did you find out?"

"A week ago."

"And you waited this long to tell me?" She was teasing, Abby heard in her voice.

"Hello. Christmas present. Anyway, this means that I'll be spending the summer in Tarrytown and Sleepy Hollow."

Katie pulled away a little. "Isn't that quite the coincidence, since I'll be here doing my own research." Her eyes seemed to sparkle. "And how weird, that one of my cousins will be out of town most of the summer with her husband and they need a housesitter. Or two."

"Funny how that works."

"It is." Katie smiled again. "This is the best Christmas ever."

"Technically, Christmas is tomorrow."

"Doesn't matter. It's still the best one ever. I'm basing that on scientific observation."

"Of?"

"You. And how you make me feel."

"I concur with your observations. It is the best one ever." And Abby pulled her into another kiss then released her. "Okay, now for your other present."

"What? I'm already having the best Christmas ever."

Abby laughed and took her gloves off. She put them in one coat pocket and took a small, flat package the size of a pocket notebook out of the other. It was wrapped in green paper and tied with a thin gold bow.

"Damn. You're even super-talented with the gift-wrapping." Katie pulled her own gloves off and shoved them inside her coat. She gently took the package from Abby and carefully opened it. "Oh, my God. It's beautiful." She ran her fingers over the cover of the chapbook. "The Secrets of Sleepy Hollow," she read. "By Tabitha Crane with inspiration from Katrina McClaren." She moved her gaze to Abby's. "Why is my name on here?"

"The theories are as much yours as mine."

Katie opened to the first page. She turned each one. "This is amazing. Everything about it is beautiful. The paper, the cover—did you handwrite this yourself or did some calligraphic master help you out?"

Abby laughed. "I did it. Calligraphy's a hobby."

"And book-making?"

"Well, yes. I do a bit of that, too. The history geek in me."

"All of these things I'm finding out about you." Katie's expression was a mixture of wonder and pleasure, and her reaction was all the thanks Abby needed. "This is...I don't have the words." Katie turned another page. "I love how you've totally re-done the legend with our theories in the style of Irving. Fortunately not exactly like him, though." She grinned. "That might get tedious."

"They did get wordy back in the day. It would've taken me three times as long and I would have needed way more paper to mimic him completely."

"This is truly beyond imagining." Katie closed the book and ran her fingers reverently over the cover. "And I'm going to read every single word as soon as I can. But right now, I don't want to miss any time with you." She leaned in and kissed Abby, and Katie's mouth was soft and tender and sent warmth rolling like a slow ocean wave through every part of Abby's body.

"Mmm." Katie pulled away. "Okay, my turn." She put the chapbook and wrapping paper in her coat pocket then took out a small box wrapped in bright red paper.

Abby removed the paper to reveal a small polished wooden box. "I already love the box."

"Keep going."

Abby opened it. A silver chain that held a silver medallion the size of a quarter nested on a piece of black cloth within. She took it out and held it so she could see what was etched on the medallion.

"A family crest?" She looked at Katie for confirmation.

"Yes. The Van Tassel. Turn it over."

Abby did. A different crest was on that side and her eyes widened. "How did you manage to get this?" She ran her thumb over the lines of the Crane family crest. "I only took it out that once when you visited me last month—" She stopped and laughed. "Duh. You took pictures."

"I did. I knew I wanted to do something with the crests, but I wasn't sure what. It came to me on the drive back to

Binghamton and fortunately, I know a few people here who do this kind of work all the time." She grinned.

"I love it." Abby flipped the medallion back to the Van Tassel crest. The clasp that attached the medallion to the chain was designed to rotate, so she could wear the medallion with either crest showing. "I love it so much." She closed her fingers around it and hugged Katie hard, wondering why she felt like crying.

"Merry Christmas," Katie said.

"You're right. This is absolutely the best Christmas ever."

"For now." Katie tucked a strand of Abby's hair into her winter cap. "Until the next one. And the ones after that."

Abby held Katie's gaze, her heart pounding. "What are you saying?"

Katie cleared her throat and smiled, though it seemed nervous. "Okay, I'm saying that I know it's only been a couple of months since we met, but I'm pretty sure I'm totally falling for you. I don't quite have all the evidence gathered yet, but some things, as you know, are beyond science." She said the words in a rush and Abby smiled. She felt like she was floating, and the only thing that kept her in place were Katie's hands on her hips.

"I am so glad." Abby slid her arms around Katie's neck and kissed her until they both were nearly breathless.

"You know what this means," Katie said against Abby's lips.

"That I'm way into you, too?"

"Okay, that. But we also appear to have proven that it's impossible for a Van Tassel to resist a Crane."

"Or vice versa."

"Fortunately." Katie grinned and Abby realized that it had started to snow again, big, fat flakes that floated lazily to the ground. Katie looked up at the sky then back at Abby. "We'd probably better head out." Katie put her gloves back on.

Abby placed the necklace back in its box and put it in her pocket. She pulled her gloves on, too, and took Katie's hand. "I'm glad I finally got you alone in the glen," Abby said. "Even if we didn't see the horseman, whether human or not."

"There will be lots of other opportunities. We're all about scientific inquiry, after all." Katie started walking and Abby had to stay a little behind her, though she was still able to hold Katie's hand. On a whim, she looked back over her shoulder. Something seemed to move on the path behind them several yards back, an amorphous shape just visible through the snow.

Abby started to say something, then stopped and continued walking. The snow was playing tricks on her. She looked back again and the shape seemed to coalesce, a big black horse and a dark headless rider, and then it was gone. Chills that had nothing to do with the cold raced up Abby's spine. The wind picked up and, where Abby thought she'd seen the apparition, blew the snow into swirls that danced on its currents.

"Hold on," Abby said. "I think I saw something."

Katie stopped and they stared for a while down the path, until the snow started to fall a little harder and the wind shifted. Abby stamped her feet a few times to warm them up. Nothing. Just the snow and the trees, whose leafless limbs looked as if they were reaching for unsuspecting passersby. Abby shivered.

"What was it?" Katie asked.

"Probably shadows and snow."

Katie's expression turned thoughtful. "Or not. There are some things science can't explain."

"I thought it looked like the horseman."

"Maybe our resident Hessian was verifying that there is, in fact, an honest-to-god Crane back in Sleepy Hollow."

Abby laughed, still a little unsettled. "I'm sure Katrina already let him know."

Katie smiled and started walking. Abby followed about a half-step behind, still holding Katie's hand. Snowflakes clung to Katie's hat and the collar of her barn jacket, and Abby thought about legends and history and how sometimes, the two were almost indistinguishable. Katie picked up the pace and soon, her SUV was visible through the snow.

"My brother is probably already trying to build up a stash of snowballs at Lu's," Katie said as they approached the vehicle, the last one parked here. The snow had already mostly covered the tracks of the others. "How are you at snowball fights?" Katie asked as she waited for Abby to get into the passenger seat.

"Guess we'll find out."

Katie grinned and went around to the driver's side and got in. "I like this Girl Scout in training thing you have going on." She started the engine and adjusted the heat. "And I really like that you're here with me. It's like having you home." Katie held Abby's gaze for a few moments and Abby saw in Katie's eyes the warm familiarity that she'd felt since the first time she'd seen her at the pub, and she knew that this was where she needed to be. Had Elizabeth felt it, too, when she first saw Katrina? Had she felt the pull of Sleepy Hollow? Probably, Abby thought. And some day, she hoped to prove it.

Katie backed up a bit then put the SUV into drive, keeping the speed down.

Abby reached into her coat pocket that contained the box with her necklace. She held onto it as Katie drove, and its surface seemed warm against her palm. "Maybe I am home," she said as she watched Katie's profile.

"I like to think so."

Abby played with Katie's hair with her free hand and watched the snow hurl itself against the front of the car. She was glad they didn't have far to go, and sure enough, about ten minutes later Katie pulled up in front of Lu's. A couple of cars Abby recognized from the night before were parked in front.

"Ready for another evening of crazy?" Katie squeezed Abby's hand.

"As long as you're around, yes."

Katie kissed her and Abby thought, not for the first time, about pulling her into the back seat for a while. Instead, she opened her door.

"Don't get me started." Abby gave her a quick kiss on the cheek and got out before she changed her mind about the back seat. "Family business first." Abby shut the door, realizing that she'd just lumped herself in with Katie's family, like she was already part of it.

"I'm going to hold you to that," Katie said as she joined Abby on the front walk.

"I'm counting on it."

Katie stared at her for a moment, and her smile made Abby's stomach flip. "Have I mentioned how much I love this story?"

"Once or twice."

"Just checking. Let's add another chapter." She took Abby's hand and even through her glove Abby thought she felt a pleasurable little current.

"Let's." Abby followed Katie up the walk, thinking about stories and their staying power, and when Katie smiled at her before they went inside, Abby knew she had found her way home.

Author's Note

Washington Irving's "The Legend of Sleepy Hollow," was published in 1820 as part of the collection *The Sketchbook of Geoffrey Crayon, Gent.* "Sleepy Hollow" is regarded as America's first literary ghost story, and became ingrained in American folklore and pop culture, spawning re-tellings and, later, movies. The tale of the headless horseman also became practically synonymous with Halloween, though Irving himself did not mention Halloween in the story because the holiday wasn't celebrated widely in the United States and wouldn't be for a hundred years after its publication.

The village in Irving's story, named "Sleepy Hollow," was North Tarrytown, which renamed itself Sleepy Hollow in 1996 as part of an economic revitalization movement. Irving first went to Tarrytown, New York (located about 25 miles from midtown Manhattan along the banks of the Hudson River) in 1798 at the age of 15, when New York City was in the midst of a yellow fever epidemic. Irving stayed with a friend while in Tarrytown, and was exposed to the area's folklore, including rumors about a headless Hessian soldier buried near the Old Dutch Church. The ghostly horseman would ride to the sites of battles in search of his head.

"The Legend of Sleepy Hollow," set in the 1790s, tells the story of schoolteacher Ichabod Crane, who is attracted to

Katrina van Tassel, daughter of Baltus van Tassel, a wealthy local farmer. Irving paints Crane as arrogant and awkward, and physically unattractive. But nevertheless, Ichabod vies for Katrina's attentions with Abraham van Brunt (known as "Brom Bones"), the town thug. (I use the English language conventions for the Dutch "van" throughout, lowercasing it when the first name is present, capitalizing it otherwise.)

One night, Crane receives an invitation to a party and he goes, hoping to win the affections of Katrina. He leaves the party and heads home on his horse. At this point, he encounters the terrifying headless horseman, who it was said could not cross a certain bridge in the area—near the church where his body was buried. Ichabod heads for that bridge, the horseman in hot pursuit, and when Ichabod crosses the bridge, he reins his horse to a stop and looks back. At that point, the horseman throws his head at Ichabod, and it hits him "in the cranium," as Irving tells it. Ichabod falls off his horse, which runs away and is found the next morning without a saddle or rider. Crane's body was never found, but his hat was, in the brook underneath the bridge, along with a shattered pumpkin.

Irving leaves the reader wondering whether it really was a ghostly headless Hessian who confronted Ichabod that night, but he also hints that Brom Bones may have masqueraded as the horseman to scare Ichabod out of town, leaving Katrina for him alone to pursue.

Though the story is largely fictional, it does rely on some actual elements. The Old Dutch Burying Ground still exists in Sleepy Hollow, but the bridge does not, though a smaller bridge was built in the cemetery in its honor. There is also a sign noting where the real bridge was. Irving may have based his characters on actual people, including a schoolteacher named Jesse Merwin from Kinderhook, where Irving had spent time in 1809. Irving may have taken the name Ichabod Crane for his schoolteacher from a captain in the Army with whom Irving served. Katrina van Tassel's character may have been based on Eleanor van Tassel Brush, and Irving might have based the name "Katrina" on Eleanor's aunt, Catriena Ecker van Texel. Brom Bones may have been based on the local blacksmith in the area at the time, Abraham Martling.

My story, "The Secret of Sleepy Hollow," takes its own liberties with the setting (largely fictionalized) and local history. I used Irving's story as a linchpin to create an alternative history in which the characters Katrina van Tassel and Ichabod Crane play important roles in one woman's search—over two hundred years later—for the truth behind Crane's disappearance.

You can read "The Legend of Sleepy Hollow" at Project Gutenberg.

Happy Halloween.

Andi Marquette, 2015

About Andi Marquette

Andi Marquette is a native of New Mexico and Colorado and an award-winning mystery, science fiction, and romance writer. She also has the dubious good fortune to be an editor who spent 15 years working in publishing, a career track that sucked her in while she was completing a doctorate in history. She is co-editor of *Skulls and Crossbones: Tales of Women Pirates* and *All You Can Eat. A Buffet of Lesbian Erotica and Romance.* Her most recent novels are *Day of the Dead*, the Goldie-nominated finalist *The Edge of Rebellion*, and the romance *From the Hat Down*, a follow-up to the novella *From the Boots Up*, a Rainbow Award runner-up.

When she's not writing novels, novellas, and stories or co-editing anthologies, she serves as both an editor for Luna Station Quarterly, an ezine that features speculative fiction written by women and as co-admin of the popular blogsite Women and Words. When she's not doing that, well, hopefully she's managing to get a bit of sleep.

CONNECT WITH THIS AUTHOR:
Website: http://andimarquette.com/

Other Books from Ylva Publishing

www.ylva-publishing.com

Caged Bird Rising

A Grim Tale of Women, Wolves, and other Beasts

Nino Delia

ISBN: 978-3-95533-319-5
Length: 237 pages (62,000 words)

In a world dominated by men, it should be Robyn's greatest fortune that the handsome Hunter Wolfmounter sees her as the perfect fertile wife. But an encounter with a mysterious wolf changes her worldview. She flees into the woods, where she meets Gwen, who helps her to change— into one of the independent beasts she has always been warned about. But the men are hot on her trail.

Banshee's Honor

Shaylynn Rose

ISBN: 978-3-95533-103-0
Length: 379 pages (153,000 words)

Warleader—in Y'Dan, this is a title of pride, of honor, and of joy. Oathbreaker—a word branded only on those whose crimes are so heinous, all must know of their crime. Both of these names have been given to Azhani Rhu'len. Only one of them is right.

Coming from Ylva Publishing

www.ylva-publishing.com

The Tea Machine

Gill McKnight

The story of a love that never dies...except it does, over and over again.

London 1862, and Millicent Aberly, spinster by choice, has found her future love—in the future! She meddled with her brother's time machine and has been catapulted into an alternative world where the Roman Empire has neither declined nor fell. In fact, it has gone on to annex most of the known universe.

Millicent is rescued from Rome's greatest enemy, the giant space squid, by Sangfroid, a tough and wily centurion who, unfortunately, dies while protecting her. Wracked by guilt and a peculiar fascination for the woman soldier, Millicent is determined to return in time and save Sangfroid from her fatal heroics. Instead, she finds her sexy centurion in her own timeline. And Sangfroid is not alone; several stowaways have come along with her.

Soon Millicent's mews house is overrun with Roman space warriors and giant squid.

Driving me Mad

L.T. Smith

For Rebecca Gibson, her journey to a work convention will be one she'll never forget. After driving around for four hours, Rebecca stops to ask for directions at an isolated house on the outskirts of Kirk Langley, Derbyshire.

Her initial meeting with the house's attractive owner, Annabel Howell, seems strange and unsettling, but at her hostess's insistence, Rebecca spends the night.

Plagued by nightmares, Rebecca senses that her dream world has blended with what she believes is reality. When she leaves the next day, her life has changed.

Can Rebecca solve a mystery that has been haunting a family for over sixty years? Will she find love along the way?

Or will the events drive her mad?

The Secret of Sleepy Hollow
© 2015 by And Marquette

ISBN: 978-3-95533-515-1

Also available as e-book.

Published by Ylva Publishing, legal entity of Ylva Verlag, e.Kfr.

Ylva Verlag, e.Kfr.
Owner: Astrid Ohletz
Am Kirschgarten 2
65830 Kriftel
Germany

www.ylva-publishing.com

First edition: October 2015

Credits
Edited by Astrid Ohletz & Joanie Bassler
Cover Design & Printlayout by Streetlight Graphics